A CUT ABOVE: THE JOHNSONS INTEGRATE LEDROIT PARK

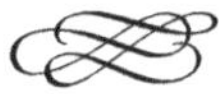

KIANNA ALEXANDER

This book is licensed to you for your personal enjoyment only.

This is a work of fiction. Names, characters, places, and incidents are either products of the writer's imagination or are used fictitiously and are not to be construed as real. Any resemblance to actual events, locales, organizations, or persons, living or dead, is entirely coincidental.

A Cut Above: The Johnsons Integrate LeDroit Park
Copyright © 2025 by Kianna Alexander
Ebook ISBN: 9781641973229
POD ISBN Trade Paperback Edition: 9781641973243
POD ISBN Hardcover Edition: 9781641973250

NYLA Publishing
121 W 27th St., Suite 1201, New York, NY 10001
http://www.nyliterary.com

as a community investor and savvy businesswoman.
Josephine's moving struggle to build family and fortune will
strike a chord in a story that is both timely and timeless—
Carolina Built is an exuberant celebration of Black women's
joy as well as their achievements!"
—**Kate Quinn,** *New York Times* **bestselling author of** *The*
Rose Code

"In Kianna Alexander's moving *Carolina Built,* readers are
afforded a look at the life of newly emancipated Josephine
Leary and her courageous efforts to build a real estate business in post-Civil War North Carolina, all the while
balancing the ever-increasing demands of her traditional
responsibilities."
— **Marie Benedict,** *New York Times* **bestselling author**
of *The Mystery of Mrs. Christie* **and** *Her Hidden Genius*

"A beautiful, heartfelt story of an extraordinary woman too
long forgotten to history. Kianna Alexander has recreated
Josephine Leary's life with wonderful historical detail and
obvious care that shines through on the page. Josephine's
strength, determination, and ambition will an inspiration to
any woman."
—**Julia Kelly, international bestselling author of** *The Last*
Garden in England

"*Carolina Built* is an integral addition to a part of our history
that omits the accomplishments of Black women. Filled with
passion and perseverance, Josephine Leary is frankly a
woman that everyone should know."
—**Sadeqa Johnson, International bestselling author**
of *Yellow Wife*

"*Carolina Built* brings to light another hidden figure whose

story is long overdue. I loved meeting Josephine Leary between these pages, the woman who moved from bondage to freedom to financial independence. Filled with dreams and passion, Josephine desired nothing more than to leave a legacy for the generations to follow—and she accomplished that. What a feat for a woman who started with nothing. Her passion and perseverance was so impressive and from the very first page, I never wanted to put this book down."
—**Victoria Christopher Murray**, *New York Times* **best-selling author of** *The Personal Librarian*

"I'm so thankful Kianna Alexander has magnificently resurrected the life and work of Josephine Leary, an entrepreneurial warrior whose guiding light is needed now more than ever. Leary's brilliant legacy in the business world, as richly depicted by Alexander in *Carolina Built*, made me cry, clap, and cheer, leaving me fully empowered to follow the pioneering path Leary forged for all to follow."
—**Piper Huguley, author of** *Sweet Tea*

"Kianna Alexander builds an intimate portrait of an ambitious woman who found a way to become more than the name, Mrs. Leary. This is not simply a wife-of-tale or the woman-behind-the-man story. Alexander deftly crafts a character-driven narrative that allows Josephine to shine, making her both remarkable and relatable. I wish to sit and have coffee with 'Jo' on her porch and listen to her wisdom of how she succeeded, how she became more—stretching her arms wide enough to hold on to her dreams, her marriage, and manage motherhood."
— **Vanessa Riley, author of** *Island Queen*

"A powerful love letter to the grit and determination of real estate maven Josephine Napoleon Leary, a formerly enslaved

African-American woman undeterred by the poverty, sexism, and racism of late-1800s North Carolina, that both satisfies and inspires."
—**Kaia Alderson, author of *Sisters in Arms***

"*Carolina Built* by Kianna Alexander tells the inspiring story of the real-life historical figure Josephine Napoleon Leary, the North Carolina former slave but free wife and mother who eventually becomes a real estate tycoon. A character-driven tale, *Carolina Built* delves expertly into the daily life of a woman whose small battles provide as much texture and passion as her and her husband's entrepreneurial ambition. It's a thrill to read a novel about a Black woman who is as successful in business as she is a wife and mother, especially in a story told in the South during the post-Civil War decades."
—**Denny Bryce, author of *Wild Women* and *The Blues***

"A triumph! *Carolina Built* shines by perfectly capturing the perseverance, grit and heart of a formidable woman who builds an empire against unbelievable odds."
—**Joanna Shupe, *USA Today* bestselling author**

"Incredibly well researched and filled with historical detail, Carolina Built is inspiring and relatable, and oftentimes humorous…. The author's passion for telling Josephine's story is evident in the pages, and I enjoyed learning about such a determined woman."
— ***Historical Novel Society***

"A pleasant panorama of middle-class small-town life in the late 19th century."
— ***Kirkus Reviews***

"Alexander's exhaustive research and the ample historical detail do justice to the material…the author does a nice job illuminating the life of an extraordinary historical figure."
— *Publishers Weekly*

"Kianna Alexander brought the real Josephine Leary to life in her page-turning book of historical fiction that leapt off the page."
—*The Southern Bookseller Review*

"A necessary addition to the literature on post–Civil War life for freed Black men and women, and a critical reminder of the power of the freedom to dream."
—*Bookreporter*

ALSO BY KIANNA ALEXANDER

STAND-ALONE TITLES

Carolina Built

Can't Resist Her

Can't Let Her Go

Drifting to You

A Radiant Soul

Working Overtime

A San Diego Romance

The Object of His Obsession

IDEAL ARRANGEMENTS

Down for Three

Three Day Weekend

Third Time's the Charm

QUEEN CITY GENTS

Lush Life

Embraceable You

Moonglow

Stardust

CLIMAX CREEK

Seducing Sheri (Book 1)

Vying for Vivian (Book 2)

Adoring Ava (Book 3)

Persuading Patrice (Book 4)

Love and Life in Climax Creek (The Complete Series)

404 SOUND

After Hours Redemption

After Hours Attraction

After Hours Temptation

What Happens After Hours

After Hours Agenda

THE SOUTHERN GENTLEMEN

Back to Your Love

Couldn't Ask for More

Never Let Me Go

SAPPHIRE SHORES

A Love Like This

Love for All Time

Forever with You

Then Came You

PHOENIX FILES

Darkness Rising

Embrace the Night

Midnight's Serenade

Love's Holiday

ROSES OF RIDGEWAY

Kissing the Captain

The Preacher's Paramour

Loving the Lawman

Electing to Love

PASSIONATE PROTECTORS

Enticed

Enchanted

Enraptured

KIANNA ALEXANDER

A CUT ABOVE

The Williamses Integrate LeDroit Park

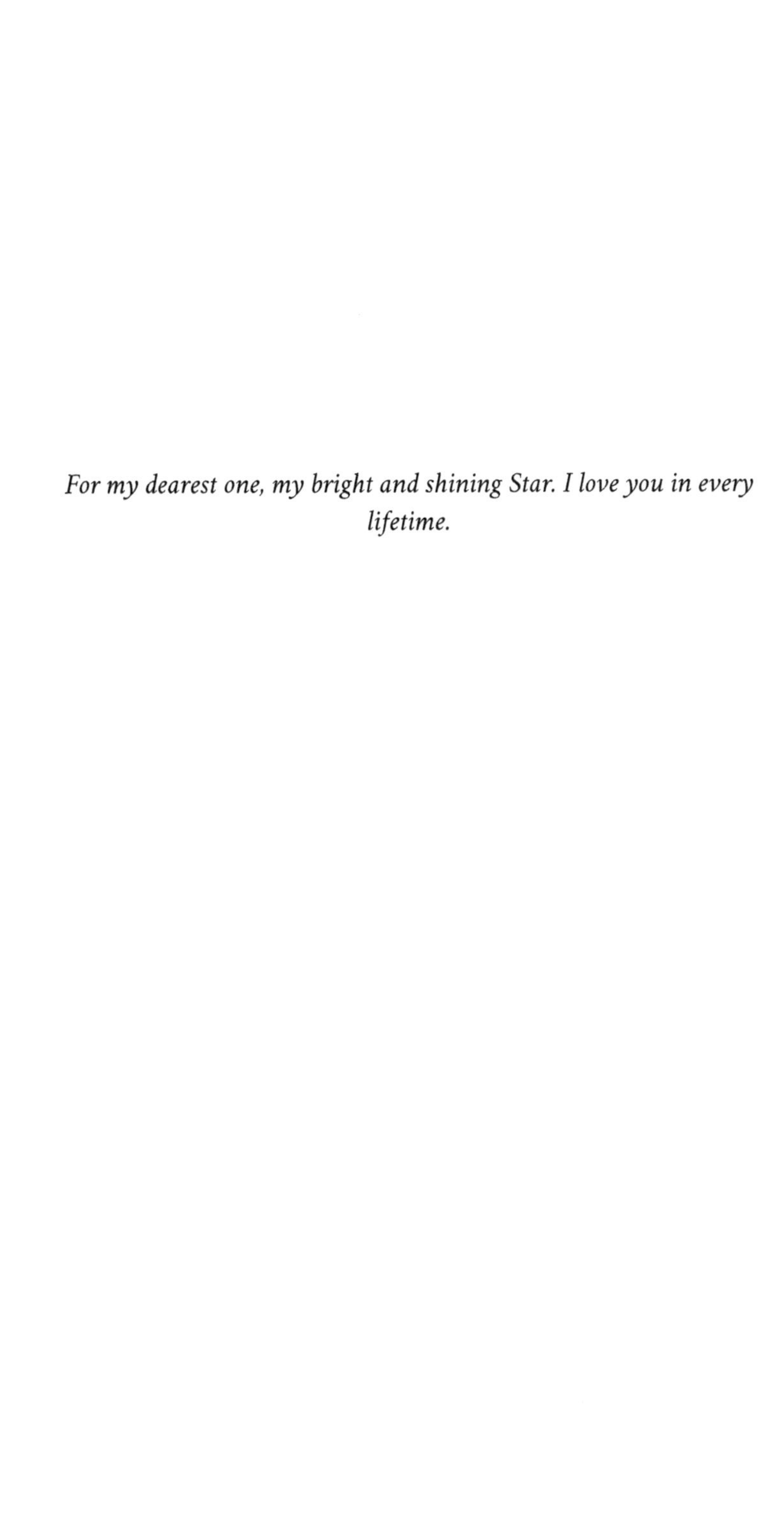

For my dearest one, my bright and shining Star. I love you in every lifetime.

--------------- ✦ ---------------

"And so, lifting as we climb, onward and upward we
go, struggling and striving, and hoping that the buds
and blossoms of our desires will burst into glorious
fruition 'ere long. With courage, born of success
achieved in the past, with a keen sense of the
responsibility which we shall continue to assume, we
look forward to a future large with promise and hope."

-Mary Church Terrell

--------------- ✦ ---------------

PROLOGUE

$\mathcal{A}$s the sun began to set on a balmy summer evening, John Jackson moved with sure strides, careful to keep up with his compatriots. The warm air, thick with humidity, though it didn't compare to those miserable, sticky nights he'd experienced back home in Texas. Whether it was the temperature or the evening's plan that had him perspiring like a sinner in a confessional, he didn't know; whatever the case, he felt as if he were melting. Dabbing his brow with a handkerchief, he tucked it away into the pocket of his denim pants.

John's older brother, Abraham, trailed a few steps behind him. Abraham's attention seemed focused elsewhere, indicated by the faraway look in his eyes.

"Come on, old man," John teased. "We don't want to get left behind because you're gathering wool."

Annoyance flashing briefly over his face, Abraham picked up his pace, closing the gap. "Hush, brother. Twenty is far from an old man."

"It's closer to old than eighteen," John chided, with a slight dig of his elbow into Abe's side.

Abraham feigned a grimace. "Get focused, youngster."

John chuckled as he returned his focus to those ahead of them in the small crowd. Charles Bane and his ragtag, cobbled-together posse of students and faculty from the Howard Institute, as well as few like-minded locals, strode purposefully through the semi-quiet streets of Washington, D.C. Their goal, the awful thing they meant to destroy, lay less than a block ahead.

Abraham's voice broke into his thoughts. His voice low, he asked, "Are we sure about following this white man? Those dandies beyond the fence aren't going to welcome us."

"We can't stand for such treatment," John replied. "We have just as much right to walk these streets as anyone else. Besides, it's troublesome to go around it all the time... it makes my treks around campus so tedious."

"Right! Down with segregation!" Abe raised a fist in the air.

John felt his resolve strengthen as they moved through the dimly lit streets, guided by the gas lamps along the road's edge. Soon, the object of their ire came into view: the old iron fence along Linden Street, that separated the haves from the have-nots. It was a blight, an insult, a thing placed there by the white folks on the other side, whose sole motivation was to make sure colored folks could never enter their little enclave.

Why would they build their precious homes so close to a Black institution, only to bar us from entering? I, for one, have had enough.

Bane stopped at the old gate and wheeled around to face those who'd accompanied him. "Waggaman's given us a simple task, fellows. We're to get rid of this damned fence!" He raised his hand and waved it about, brandishing the trusty crowbar in his fist.

A roar of agreement erupted among the small but determined assemblage, and a moment later, they descended on the fence like a swarm of locusts covering a crop. The sounds of their shouts filled the air, mingling with the distinctive clang of metal striking metal and the thumps and thuds of fence parts being flung to the ground.

Abe was upon the structure in a flash, using their father's old smithing hammer to damage the fence. John joined him a few moments later. As he scraped his small handsaw back and forth over one of the joints, he let his frustration have its head.

I'm a good, upstanding citizen, a learned man, a hard worker. Why should I be kept out of a place like Ledroit Park? Why aren't I good enough to walk these streets or to build my home there?

"Hey!" An angry shout rose from within the bounds of LeDroit Park, the promised land that lay beyond the fence. "What the hell are you doing?"

"Never you mind," Bane called back, still prying at a stubborn post. "Keep at it, boys."

The group continued their task until one among them pointed and hollered. "Look!"

John scanned the horizon beyond the fence, and gasped. A group of men marched toward them, shoulder to shoulder. Many held aloft their rifles and handguns; other, clubs and other instruments of pain. A few had donned the familiar white garments that reminded him of unspeakable horrors and burning crosses back home in Texas.

Bane saw them too, and ceased his work, slowly backing away.

From among the defenders, a shot rang out, the boom piercing the air.

The man who'd pointed fell, and John stood frozen in horror as Bane and another fellow scooped up his limp form.

Did he faint? Or is he...

Another shot rang out as the terrible, ghostly assemblage drew closer to the fence.

Abe grabbed John's arm and tugged. "Run, brother!"

The fence breakers scattered, leaving behind a bent and listing pile of rubble, metal bars and fittings as they disappeared into the darkness.

A CUT ABOVE

The Williamses Integrate LeDroit Park

CHAPTER 1

-Octavius-

17 March 1880
Franklyn, Southampton County, Virginia

Octavius stood by the window of his room in the Myers Hotel, looking out on the beautiful spring day. The lush green of the cleared land surrounding the two-story structure stretched out like a vibrant carpet, giving way to deeper, verdant blues and greens of the forest beyond. Pines and spruce reached their branches toward an unblemished swath of blue sky.

He lifted the sash to let a little fresh air in, inhaling the sweet scent of blooming magnolia and freshly trimmed grass. Moving away from the window, he found himself returning to the looking glass once more. The dark gray jacket and trousers, fashioned of lightweight but sturdy material by Eunice Fitz, Edenton's best seamstress, looked quite striking with the white shirt beneath. He'd foregone a necktie, in favor of a handily tied scarf about his neck; a wedding gift from his brother-in-law and coworker, Sweety.

His appearance in the glass pleased him, and he smiled, choosing not to fuss with the scarf lest he ruin the effect.

A knock sounded on the door. His smile deepened as he recognized the soft voice. "Come in, Mother."

Jeanette opened the door, but instead of entering the room, she merely wedged her body into the opening. "Son, it's time for you to come out to the garden."

"Why don't you come in?" He could see the sheen of tears dancing in her eyes.

"Because I've already been to see Missy, and if I come in there with you, I'll bawl for sure, and I'll ruin my face paint."

Chuckling at his mother's plainspoken honesty, he said, "I'll be along directly."

With a nod, she slipped out, leaving the door ajar.

As promised, he gathered his senses and the box containing the golden band, and got himself downstairs and out the back door to the garden.

He strolled down the aisle between the two rows of chairs, greeting the thirty or so who'd assembled to witness the blessed event with a simple nod or wave as he passed. He stopped next to the good Reverend James, taking his place beneath the pergola, which had been festooned with a garland of flowers and ivy.

He looked to the doorway as a hush fell over the assemblage, and he grinned at the sight of his five-year-old niece, Clara, as she appeared in the doorway. She paraded down the aisle in her frilly pink dress, scattering petals along the path in a manner than could only be described as theatric. He resisted the urge to pinch her cheek as she settled into a chair next to her mother, his sister Josephine.

He glanced back toward the door, and his breath left him when he caught sight of Missouri.

My Lord in Heaven. What a sight she is.

She was a beautiful and radiant as an angel, with the gossamer white fabric floating around her, shimmering like wings in the sunlight. He shifted his weight from side to side as she made her slow, graceful approach, impatient for her to reach him. When she finally did, he took her hands in his and gazed into her eyes.

"You're a vision," he whispered.

Her soft smile lit his entire world. They turned to the minister, and the ceremony passed in a blur of exhilaration and joy. Once vows were exchanged and prayers sent up, Reverend James announced them as man and wife. Josephine assisted their sage grandmother, Milly, in carrying an ornate broom to the altar. Grandma Milly defied her seven decades of living and knelt low, holding the broom aloft so that he and his new bride could take the sacred leap, representing their transition into a new life of love and togetherness. Once their feet were on the ground again, he wasted no time in grabbing Missouri up in his embrace and kissing her lips.

The assemblage moved deeper into the hotel's large garden, where a wedding supper had been laid out for them. Two trestle tables in the grass held the victuals; Dutch oven-roasted chicken, turnips, collard greens, thick slices of corn-pone, and Milly's apple brown betty. Smaller tables were scattered about the area for guests to eat and socialize, and he took in the sight, appreciating all the effort that had gone into putting the affair together, as he escorted his wife to the table set up for them beneath a whitewashed pergola.

Josephine arrived at the table not long after they'd sat down, her eyes dancing with tears. "Oh, it was just beautiful. Congratulations, little brother."

He reached for his sister's hand and gave it a squeeze. "Thanks, Jo. Goodness, you and Mama puddle up at the slightest thing."

She dabbed at her eyes with a handkerchief. "Marriage is nothing slight, I assure you." She sighed. "I only wish Sweety could have come. But it was so good of him to stay home and mind the baby so I could be here to see my only brother get married..." she paused, grasping Missouri's hand with her free one, "and so I could welcome my new sister into the family."

Missouri held Josephine's hand for a moment, then broke the contact as she got up and circled the table. Next he knew, both his wife and sister were openly weeping and embracing each other.

Goodness. He'd never quite understood the female mind and their insistence on emotional shows, but he let them have at it nonetheless.

I haven't made twenty-one yet, but I know enough to let them carry on as they see fit, if I want to live a long and peaceful life.

-Missouri-

Missy felt the tears streaming down her face as she hugged Josephine tight. She finally pulled back, mindful of their fancy garments. "Oh, I'm sorry, Jo. My face paint has made a mess of your shoulder."

Josephine dabbed at her own eyes as she stepped back, then used the handkerchief to wipe at the colorful splotches dotting the jacket of her pink summer weight traveling costume. "Never you mind, Missy. If I hadn't already cried all mine off, your dress would be besmirched, too."

They were laughing at their own overflowing emotions when a small voice interrupted their amusement. "Mama, when do we get to have cake?" Missy's gaze settled on little Clara, who was excitedly tugging the side of her mother's skirt to get her attention.

Josephine squatted down and spoke to her daughter.

"Now, Clara. You must eat some real food before you can have cake. And do you remember what I told you about wedding suppers and who has cake first?"

Clara nodded, her thick ribbon-tipped pigtails swaying in time with the motion. "Yes. The gride and broom get to have cake first, then everybody else after them."

Missy stifled a giggle. "Clara, you must be the sweetest little girl ever to be born."

Josephine patted her head. "That's close enough, my darling. Now go and sit with Great Granny Milly. I'll be over there in a bit, alright?"

"Yes, Mama." The child bounded off, looking every bit like a small pink confection with limbs.

"Who dressed her for today?" Missouri asked. "She looks so precious."

"Well, Mrs. Fitz made the dress, of course. Mama and I wrestled her into it this morning, and Grandma Milly's the one who put all those pretty ribbons in her hair and got her into her fancy slippers." Josephine blew out a breath. "My child is a ball of energy. We had such a time getting her dressed."

"Well, the effect was worth the effort, Jo." She gave her shoulder a squeeze. "Ever since I started courting Octavius, you've always made me feel welcome. I must say...it feels good to have such a fine sister."

Josephine placed a glove covered hand to her heart. "Oh, land's sake. Let me go look after my child before you start me to cryin' again." She pecked her on the cheek, then slipped away to locate Clara.

Hearing someone clear their throat, Missy turned toward the sound and smiled.

"Could I have an audience with my new wife?" Octavius' sly question was accompanied by a wicked grin spread across his face.

She eased closer to his side and let herself be enfolded as his strong arms circled her waist, pulling her flush with his side. "We haven't been married an hour...don't tell me you're already getting possessive."

He gave her a squeeze. "Always, my love. I want as much of your attention and time as I can get." His crooked finger beneath her chin tilted her head up, and they stared into each other's eyes for a moment before their lips met.

The bell-like tinkling of metal upon glass cut through the mist of love, bringing Missy's attention back to the present. Octavius eased away from her, offering a sly wink. She smiled, turning toward their hostess, her aunt Clotilda, who stood in the center of the garden, tapping her drinking glass with a fork.

"Attention, everyone. Thank you for coming to our blessed event, my niece's marriage." A smattering of applause occurred. "Now, if you will, please proceed to the food tables and serve yourselves, so we can get our wedding supper underway."

The guests began lining up to get their food, while the newlyweds took their seats. In short order, Aunt Clotilda and one of her friends appeared at the table, placing bountiful plates and filled glasses of lemonade in front of them. After accepting a peck on the cheek from her aunt as the two older women departed, Missy looked at the plate in awe. "Goodness, how am I to eat all this? This plate is more suited for a soldier going off to war."

Her husband, already forking up a helping of greens, shook his head. "You must eat, my love. Even if you can't finish it. Trust me—"He paused, his eyes dancing with the promise of things both wicked and pleasurable. "You will need your strength."

She reached for the pearl buttons at her throat and loosened the top one, hoping to let some of the steam escape as she considered the repercussions of his words. Mindful of the occasion and the mixed company, she left the button open only for a moment before refastening it, removing her white lace gloves, and digging into her meal.

Later, with the merriment in full swing, she gazed into her husband's eyes as he twirled her around the garden for their first dance. Aunt Clotilda, in her typical well-connected way, had gotten a violinist for the event, and as they waltzed over the vacant patch of soft grass centering the garden to the tune of Sullivan's "My Dearest Heart," she felt as if she and her husband had sprouted wings and were dancing upon air. The words to the tune were as fitting as she could imagine, and she heard them in her mind as the musician played.

> *"All the dreaming is broken through,*
> *Both what is done and undone I rue.*
> *Nothing is steadfast, nothing is true,*
> *But your love for me, and my love for you,*
> *My dearest, dearest heart!"*

A fresh wave of tears gathered in her eyes, and she snuggled closer to Octavius, resting her head in the recess of his strong shoulder. Nothing could compare to this man or to the deep, abiding love she felt for him and his family.

The revelry continued into the evening, and at every turn, she found herself crying happy tears. She wept when her mother-in-law, Jeanette, and her grandmother-in-law, Milly, presented her with the most beautiful lace monogrammed handkerchiefs to welcome her to the family. She puddled up when a collection was taken up among the guests for the care of her ill mother back home in South Carolina, then cried again when Clara asked her to kneel and gave her a flower she'd picked, and a kiss on the cheek.

"What's the matter, Auntie?"

Dabbing at her eyes, Missy shook her head. "Goodness. I'm just overwhelmed with love and happiness. That's all, my dear."

Satisfied with that answer, Clara bounded off across the grass.

As the sun dipped low in the sky, she and many of the gathered guests boarded the Queen of the Bay, a small ship Aunt Clotilda chartered for their cruise back home to Edenton. They set sail at dusk, and Missy looked out over the glistening water at the rising moon.

"What a beautiful day this has been." Her husband stood behind her at the window of their small cabin, his arms draped about her waist holding her close to his body.

Enjoying the warmth of him, and the smell of the fine cologne he wore combined with the subtly salty air flowing over the water, she nodded. "It was glorious."

"How do you think Sweety is faring with the baby?"

She grinned as she thought of their brother-in-law, having spent the past two days changing diapers, preparing bottles, and generally keeping their niece Florrie alive. "I'd wager his will be the first face we'll see waiting for us as the dock in Edenton Bay."

The both had a laugh, then settled into comfortable silence and the glow of love.

CHAPTER 2

-**Octavius**-

July 1888
Edenton, NC

I don't know how I missed this yesterday evening.

Broom in hand, Octavius hummed quietly as he used the straw bristles to chase a pile of fallen hair onto the flat board he used as a dustpan. At this early hour, he could actually hear himself humming; the barbershop was the quietest it would be all day.

Once Sweety opens this place, it will be chatter and carrying until we close.

His brother-in-law had gone around back to set a few mouse traps, leaving him alone inside to do the last few preparations for opening. After he'd dumped the hair, dust and whatever other debris he'd swept up into the waste bin, he returned the tools to the supply room in the back.

By the time he made it to his station, the bell over the

door chimed as Sweety strode in. "We all set for opening, 'Tavious?"

"For sure. Flip that sign," he replied.

Sweety turned the wooden sign on the door, then slipped inside and let it swing shut behind him. "There. Maybe we won't be too busy today; it's Tuesday, after all."

He chuckled. "You forgot about it, didn't you?

Brow scrunched and eyes narrowed, Sweety said, "What you talkin' about? What have I forgotten?"

"The Wilson twins. It's their eighteenth birthday." He shook his head, marveling at how his brother-in-law never seemed to keep up with the goings on in town.

Scratching his chin and appearing contemplative for a moment, Sweety finally snapped his fingers. "Oh, right. Meaning Old Man Wilson and his wife will finally let them entertain suitors."

He nodded. "Exactly. They're pretty girls, too. You're liable to see every young man in the county here today, hoping to win one favor with one sister or the other."

"It's Old Man Wilson's favor they really got to win," Sweety chided. "That's why I like having you in here, and why Jo makes me such a good wife. You Williamses are good with details."

He tipped his imaginary hat. "Coming from where we did, being resourceful was the only option."

Sweety nodded and set about tying his apron around his waist.

Sure enough, before the next half-hour elapsed, two young men showed up together. The taller, rail thin one sat with Sweety for a shave and trim, while the stouter one eased into Octavius' chair for a haircut.

While he shaped the thick, uneven curls into the requested short, professional cut, he listened to the young man, who'd introduced himself as Aaron, go on about Bonnie Wilson.

"She's a real beauty. She'll make me a fine wife," Aaron insisted. "Yes, sir."

His friend, Robert, offered a laugh from his seat in Sweety's chair. "Have at her, as long as Beatrice is left to me. She's smart as a whip, and spirited, too."

"You sure that's what you want?" Sweety posed the question as he used the straight razor to erase the whiskers along Robert's chin. "I've got a spirited one myself...they can be a handful."

Deciding not to toss a comb at Sweety for his subtle dig at his sister Jo, Octavius instead announced, "It takes a real man to handle a woman with spirit."

That seemed to hush Sweety up, because he pressed his lips together in a thin smile as the two young patrons continued to sing the praises of Old Man Wilson's precious daughters.

When Robert and Aaron took their leave, more young men replaced them, with the same goal in mind- to convince either Beatrice or Bonnie to give them a chance.

Octavius was finishing up a shy, quiet youngster who hadn't said two words his entire appointment when he glanced to the front and noticed his father-in-law sitting in one of the chairs. "Be with you shortly, Dorsey."

Engrossed in his copy of the *Fisherman and Farmer*, Dorsey threw up his hand to acknowledge Octavius' words.

"I sure hope the womenfolk are having a productive time at their conference," Sweety commented as he wiped down his countertop between clients. "Would have been nice to have Jo's help today."

He nodded. His older sister was among the few women barbers in the state, and certainly one of the most highly skilled of any persuasion. For the past week, she and most of the women of their church had been busy with their summer conference. "We'll be fine, Sweety. How many more potential husbands for the Wilson girls could there be?"

Dorsey took his turn in Octavius' chair, removing the dusty flat crowned hat he wore most days when he worked. "Thought I'd pop by and get a trim...forgot about the Wilson girls."

He chuckled. "Fitting you in is no problem, Dorsey. How are you faring without Mama there at the house?"

He offered a plaintive sigh. "She left me plenty food, no doubt. But I still miss her something fierce."

He smiled. "Does my heart good to see my Mama loved so well."

"She's a real peach, our Jeanette." Dorsey cleared his throat. "We're about done with that little cabin for the Perkins family. We could maybe fit you in before the next job, if you and Missy want to add that room on to your place."

He considered the offer, thinking of the modest cottage he shared with his wife, and how they'd talked of expanding it one day. "I don't think we're ready to be adding on just yet, Dorsey."

"Fair enough." Dorsey moved on, chatting about the next job he and his crew would take on, a project they were working on with the Badhams, a local family of highly skilled architects.

While Dorsey talked, Octavius heard every few words, and occasionally muttered his agreement here and there. Mainly though, his mind wandered to thoughts of Missy, and their quiet little place on the edge of town. He'd loved the silence of the countryside when they'd moved in, and he still did. It afforded him the privacy to demonstrate his love to Missy without fear of their carrying on being heard by anyone else. Yet, Dorsey's casual question reminded him of his aspiration of fatherhood, the dream of a home blessed with the presence of a child. He and Missy shared that dream, but so far, it had yet to come to fruition, and neither he nor his wife had any good answers as to why.

His own father was a man of the so-called superior race, who refused to even acknowledge his existence. Octavius could see no greater gift than the blessing of a child, one that would carry his name and legacy forward into the future as a free American, it was more precious than he could put to words.

For a man whose freedom was purchased with blood, nothing matters more than legacy.

-Missouri-

"Goodness gracious, it's hot."

Inhaling a deep breath of the warm, stagnant air inside one of the classrooms in the Badham School, Missouri blew a fallen curl out of her face. She knew tucking it back beneath her headscarf would be the more effective approach, but she couldn't spare a hand at the moment. The complex embroidery she was stitching demanded her full attention.

Josephine, seated to her left, nodded as she used a handkerchief to mop her glistening brow. "Hot as Hades. Good thing we're doing the Lord's work, eh?"

"Yes," Evelina, the school's headmistress and namesake, quipped. "For we obviously aren't cut out for the heat, ladies."

The dozen or so chairs in the classroom were all occupied by women of the St. John the Evangelist's Ladies Auxiliary. Each of them had a sewing project in front of her.

"Well, weather aside. this has always been my favorite part of our summer conference, " Ida Jenkins admitted. "I do love making things for the new babies."

Her twin sister Izzy grinned. "Me, too. Can you believe we've had five new babies born in the congregation, just over the last few weeks? Surely, the Lord has blessed us."

Amens and other words of agreement filled the small room, and Missouri's was among them. She kept her face impassive, though, and her eyes remained locked on the small pink flower she was adding to the stuffed doll she'd carefully pieced together. It was the fifth one she'd made over the last week; since Jo had picked up on her talent for making dolls and stuffed animals, Missouri has been repeatedly assigned that duty.

She looked at the coal black buttons she'd used for the doll's eyes, and wondered about the little girl who'd receive the doll as a gift from the Ladies' Auxiliary.

I bet the mother will put this doll in the babe's crib to watch over her at night while she sleeps and has sweet, innocent dreams.

She drew another deep breath, trying to shake off the melancholy that often beset her when she dwelled too long on thoughts of babies.

"Are you alright, Missy?" Jo touched her forearm. "Don't soldier on if you need to take a break, sister."

She mustered a smile. "No. I was just gathering wool, I'm fine. "

A companionable silence settled over the room as the ladies kept up their sewing, and Missouri glanced around at the faces of the women she counted as her friends and neighbors. They were some of the best women around, smart, capable, and kind; a credit to the race in every way. Evelina, dedicated teacher to the town's Black children and wife of the foremost architect in the region. Ida and Izzy, mother figures and tireless advocates for suffrage and civil rights. Eunice Fitz, a highly skilled seamstress. Her sister-in-law, Jo, who somehow managed to raise two daughters, run two businesses, and be a doting wife, all while still making time to offer all the sisterly love and guidance she could ever ask for.

She loved being a part of this group, and of the larger Edenton community. And while she had no special skill or trade, she filled her days being an upstanding wife and companion to Octavius, carrying out community work, and spending time with her nieces so Josephine and Sweety could have breaks. She knew what life had been like under bondage, and truly, she had no pressing complaints. She was happy, loved, and well cared for.

But is that enough for me? Deep down she knew it wasn't.

She felt a tap on her shoulder, dragging her out of the world of her thoughts and back to reality.

"Missy, I'd say that flower's about done." Jo gestured toward the doll.

Glancing down at it, she could see that the rosette was already noticeably bigger than the other ones she'd made in the doll's flower crown headband. "Oh, shoot."

Jo chuckled. "Why don't you step outside with me for a bit of fresh air?"

She set the doll on the small desk positioned in front of her and stood. "I think I'd better."

The two of them slipped out of the classroom. A short walk took them down the narrow hallway and out the propped-open back door of the schoolhouse. In the school-yard, Jo used the pump to fetch them two tumblers of water, and they sat down at one of the three picnic tables where students often had their lunch on warm days.

"So, it seems you've got that faraway look in your eyes again, sister." Jo eyed her expectantly. "What's bothering you? Is it what I think?"

Missy took a long sip, letting the cool water splash down her throat. "I suppose."

"I worried that I shouldn't put you to work on this

project, but you're so good at making dolls. No one else in the group can do it as well as you." She sighed. "You know I don't intend to upset you by asking you to put your skills to use for the little ones, right?"

"I know, Jo. And I really do enjoy helping out in this way." She set her tumbler down. "I just can't help thinking about..." She let her voice trail off.

Jo placed her hand on her shoulder and gave it a gentle squeeze. "I know. Your little one would be three years old if she were here."

Tears welled in her eyes as she felt that familiar pain, the one she doubted would ever leave her. "Losing our babe...it changed me. At times I feel I'm unraveling at the seams, Jo."

"Take heart, sister. Anyone would feel out of sorts after suffering something like that." Jo's words were gentle, but pointed. "And there's no timeline on grieving, either."

"I love Clara and Florrie so much. Being their aunt is a great joy. And I love all the little ones I mind for our friends, too. But..."

"I know, dear. You want a babe of your own."

She nodded. "And so does Octavius, bless him. He'd make a capital father." She sniffled, using the back of her hand to wipe the tears that slid down her cheek. "I think...part of the reason I've struggled so much is that I feel I failed him in a way."

"That's nonsense, Missy. You can't control the timing of things like this."

"In my head, I know that. But still, it pains me not to have babies by now, and not knowing why just makes it worse. Even Doc Trent says he could find no good reason I wasn't able to carry." She shrugged her shoulders, not knowing how else to express her deep sadness and frustration.

Jo pulled her in for a tight hug. "I don't want you worrying yourself over this, Missy. When the time is right, the Lord will bless you and 'Tavious with a sweet baby. I just know it."

As she let herself be soothed by the sister of her heart, Missouri flung another prayer heavenwards.

Please, Lord. Let Jo be right.

CHAPTER 3

-Octavius-

June 1891
Edenton, NC

*W**here am I?*

The hazy light of dawn surrounded Octavius, and he looked around, gauging his surroundings. He found himself walking through a sparse, wooded grassland, unsure of how he'd come to be there in the first place. It was a place he'd never been, yet it seemed so familiar.

The grass, slightly brown, grazed his bare ankles as the warm breeze flowed by. Short shrubs dotted the landscape, punctuating the broad spaces between the thick trunks of many baobab trees.

What is this place?

He took in the strange beauty of it, and as he started to walk, he continued to let his eyes take in as much as possible. The boundless sky above was the color of lavender blossoms, unfettered by clouds. Unable to remain still, he gave into the inexplicable urge to explore, feeling every blade of grass that gave way beneath the soles of his feet as he moved toward something in the distance.

In a small clearing, shaded beneath the fan-like branches of the baobab trees, he saw them. It was a gathering of men, standing in a semi-circle, with their backs toward him. Each man wore a brightly colored cloth of a different pattern, fashioned into a robe-like garment that covered their bodies from their necks to their ankles, leaving only one shoulder and their arms bare. He glanced down at the similar fabric wrapped and tied around his own waist, the only thing he wore; yet he felt somehow underdressed, and out of place.

As he got closer, he could hear them speaking in a tongue he didn't understand. He hung back a bit, taking up a position far enough away that he would not disturb whatever meeting they were carrying on. As he wondered what they might be discussing, the men suddenly grew quiet.

Octavius watched as five sets of dark, curious eyes turned his way. Realizing they'd seen him; he took a step back.

The man in the center of the group broke off from the rest, and began walking toward Octavius. He was not as tall as the others, but he moved with an air of importance and power. His steps, aided by an ornate wooden staff, were slow and deliberate.

Part of him wanted to run, perhaps even hide, but he found himself rooted to the spot. He swallowed, doing his best to hold on to his wits as the old man entered his personal space.

The old man gaze raked over him, sizing him up, before

settling on his face. "Why do you act as if you don't belong here?"

He stared. *I can understand him now.* "Belong? I don't even know where I am."

"Your eyes may not know this place, but a soul never forgets its home." The old man's expression remained serene.

Confused, he asked, "Why am I here?"

"To learn what you must know." The old man raised his staff in the air and then brought it down forcefully, the end striking the ground with a thump. "You must leave the home to know to make the home you need."

"What?" He balked, feeling unsettled. "Why?"

"Where you are is not where you must be." The old man began to pace, circling Octavius as he spoke. "You are afraid. These words upset you."

Octavius nodded, seeing no point in pretending otherwise.

"Become a warrior to the enemy of fear. Go where you must go, child. Only there will your legacy truly come to be."

He still didn't understand what the old man meant, or where and when this journey would begin. "Where must I to go?"

"Go to the seat where power sits. Where the pale man pretends he is king. There, plant your legacy, and it will grow." The old man ceased his pacing.

As they stood and faced each other once again, Octavius stared into the face, burnished by the sun and creased with age. There, he saw the familiar features of his mother and grandmother. He looked into the golden eyes, which held wisdom untold, and asked, "Who are you?"

"Who are *you*?" The old man parroted the question back to him, emphasizing the last word.

Before Octavius could respond, the man raised his staff

and pushed the carved lion's head handle toward him, until the knobby wood solidly struck the center of Octavius chest.

The impact startled him, his body jerked—

And he awoke in his bed, sweat beading around his hairline. Outside the window of the cottage, the sun had begun its climb over the horizon. The same hazy light filtered through the lace curtains, casting a glow upon the bed. His wife's shrouded, sleeping form occupied the space next to him.

He sat in the bed for a long time, gathering his scattered thoughts while Missy slumbered at his side.

-Missouri-

From beneath the wide brim of a flower-festooned straw hat, Missouri watched the festivities going on around her, from the perch on the back steps of St. John the Evangelist.

That Juneteenth banner turned out so nice. The children must be proud of their work.

The annual celebration of Emancipation was well underway, and the churchyard bustled with activity. Her husband and brother-in-law were playing horseshoe at the pit, the children of town dashed around, expending their boundless energy. Across the way, she spotted her sister-in-law Josephine, headed for the pit.

I suppose I'll visit with Jo. She rose from her seat on the hard stone and made her way across the grass. Tapping her shoulder, she said, "Your Sweety is quite good at horseshoes."

Josephine nodded as Sweety scored another ringer. "He's been throwing shoes since before emancipation."

"It shows."

She angled her body toward Missouri. "I love that navy skirt, dear sister-in-law."

"Thanks. I found it at Newman's store. He's got quite a

selection of colors and fabrics. Has plenty of day dresses, too."

"My only qualm is the white blouse," Jo said. "Don't you know you're likely to sully it during the festivities?"

She laughed. "Oh, go on with you, Jo. Besides, it was my only clean blouse. I'm overdue for some time at the washboard."

An awful sound, loud and rumbling, put a halt to the conversation, and she whirled toward Queen Street, seeking the source of the fracas.

A buggy, flying the old Stars and Bars, careened toward the grove, with horses' hooves thundering and wheels squeaking as the driver turned off the road. The bearing of the vehicle had it barreling straight toward the gathering.

Rooted to the spot, she heard Josephine screaming and the squeal of the children as their guardians tried to snatch them out of harm's way. Folks scrambled out of the way as the buggy flew through the center of the churchyard, toppling the tables of food and tearing through the hand-painted Juneteenth banner.

Sweety raced toward them and grabbed Josephine, and both of them toppled to the ground, out of the buggy's path.

"Take this, darkies!"

A moment after she heard those awful words, something hit her in the chest. She fell to the ground as more heavy, slimy objects pelted her like some hellish rain.

There was more rumbling and ruckus, and then, the buggy sped onto Church Street and was gone. There, seated in the grass, she looked down at herself.

And when she saw the gelatinous red flesh clinging to her clothing, she dropped her head into her hands and let herself cry. Time fell away as she let vented her emotions, tears spilling down her cheeks and dampening her collar.

She had no idea where he came from, but Octavius joined

her in the grass, and wrapped his arms around her. "Did they hurt you, my love?"

She shook her head, but the tears continued to flow, and he held her as they did.

Josephine appeared above them, breathlessly asking, "Are you hurt?"

She drew a deep, shaky breath to steady herself before she answered. "They were tomatoes. Rotten tomatoes." Missouri gestured to one of the flattened fruits lying next to her on the ground. "They rode through here like Lucifer's own minions and pelted us with rotten tomatoes." She looked to her sister-in-law as tears gathered in her eyes. "Why, Jo? Why do they do these things?"

Josephine's eyes were damp too, and she simply shook her head, as if she couldn't find the words to explain.

Octavius had no such trouble. "I'll tell you why they do it," he announced while flinging bits of tomato flesh off his denims. "They are hateful, ignorant fools, and I've grown sick of their madness." The fury flashed in his eyes, making them look like lit coals.

Josephine countered, "So am I, Octavius. But what are we to do about it?"

"I don't know what you will do, but I know what I will do." He reached out to her and she gratefully took his hand, letting him guide her to her feet. With a gentle touch that melted her like ice on a hot sidewalk, he wiped her tears. "I'll take my sweet wife away from this."

Looking at him, she felt her heart flutter. His expression was mixture of righteous anger and determination, and knowing he was so committed to protecting her made her fall in love with him all over again.

"Where will you go?" Jo asked pointedly. "And who will look after you?"

"Sis, I know you still see me as a child. But I'm thirty-two years old. I can figure it out, I can make a good life for my wife and me." He cradled her close to his side.

Jo sighed. "I'm sorry, brother. I know you're full-grown, and I know you're capable. I'd never want to make you feel as if I didn't believe in you." She wrung her hands, as she often did when fretting over something. "But I can't imagine my life without you nearby. We've been together since childhood."

Observing the exchange, Missouri realized she was of two minds on the matter. She had great respect and admiration for her husband, and she trusted him such that she would follow him anywhere. But what would become of the two of them, alone in a strange city, without the comforts of family and the community they'd built in Edenton?

Octavius drew a deep breath. "I know, Jo. And I would miss you and Mama, and Granny Milly terribly. But I simply can't stay here." He paused in his declaration, cupped his wife's chin in his hand, and kissed each of her cheeks in turn. "Look at her. I love her more than life itself. Seeing her hurt, seeing her shed tears is physically painful for me, and I won't stand by and keep subjecting her to this misery."

Missouri swallowed. *How can I be against my husband's plans, when he loves me so? I know he'd give his last breath to protect me. I vowed to spend my life at his side, and that's what I'm going to do.* Clearing her throat of the residual tightness, she said, "You know I love you, Jo. Sweety and the girls and the rest of the family, too. But it's all too much. I'm tired of these entitled white girls trying to touch my hair and their mothers pursuing me to be their housemaid. I'm tired of these perverse white men who think it's acceptable to ogle me or touch my bottom when we pass on the sidewalk." She shook her head. "I want to be a mother, and I can't see raising my child in such a place."

"And I'm tired of being followed around every store I visit

and of watching ladies clutch their purses at the mere sight of me." Octavius ran a hand over his short curls. "I've had enough. As soon as I can arrange it, I'm taking my wife north."

CHAPTER 4

-Octavius-

December 1892
Edenton, NC

Seated in the sanctuary of St. John the Evangelist, Octavius kept his arm draped around Missouri's waist. His closed Bible lay on his lap, and as he listened to the tail end of Rector Billups's sermon on divine guidance, he found the minister's words particularly relevant.

"God has ordered the events of our life, before we have even been born," Rector Billups decreed from his spot behind the carved mahogany pulpit. "We know this because scripture tells us so. Jeremiah, chapter 29, verse 11 says this: 'For I know the plans I have for you, says the Lord, plans for welfare and not for evil, to give you a future and a hope.' It recorded right there, to assure us of our destinies."

The minister paused to drink from the tumbler of water kept at his side.

Octavius took the opportunity to glance at his wife. Even in profile, and even as she wore the malaise of early pregnancy like a heavy cloak, she was still the most beautiful creature he'd ever beheld. She appeared tired, drawn, and her hastily tied bun was coming undone. Reaching over, he tightened the ribbon before her curls could break free, and the gesture earned him a radiant smile and a whisper of thanks.

"So, if we already know that the Lord has a plan for each one of us, and has set that plan in motion, then why would we ever need to worry?" The rector pushed his spectacles up on the bridge of his nose, shuffling the pages in front of him. "Our mortal concerns are but a waste of our precious time here. This life is fleeting; best we put our efforts on service to God, and to our fellow man, to piety and to prayer. Amen."

"Amen," echoed the congregation.

"Let us pray."

As the rector led the prayer, Octavius held his wife's hand tightly within his own. As he had at every opportunity since they'd discovered the blessing Missy now carried within her womb, he sent his silent but heartfelt thanks up to the heavens. In less than a year, their fondest dream would become reality, when they welcomed the child they'd prayed for since the day they wed.

Truly, you've blessed me, Lord. I thank you for my loving family. For my precious wife. And for the little one yet to come.

After another round of amens signaled the close of prayer, Sister Brownlee, who served as church clerk, took her place behind the small podium that sat to the right of the pulpit and choir stand. "Good morning, sisters and brothers. I greet you in the Lord's peace as I come to deliver the church announcements." She paused to clear her throat, then began reading from the papers she'd brought with her to the podium. "We begin with a letter from a friend of Rector

Billups, which I will read to the congregation based on his request. This letter is from Reverend John Sims, of the Universal Holiness Church in Washington D.C, and it reads thusly. 'Dear Marion, greetings from your old friend, Bishop. I hope you and your family are well and enjoying good health and the bounty of God's peace. I am writing to you with a somewhat rare and possibly strange request. In June of next year, I will retire after twenty-five years of service as barber to the U.S. House and Senate, so I can focus more on my religious work. This will leave my post at the Capitol Barber Shop vacant, and it is my wish to have another capable barber of our race to fill the post, if it can be done. I'm writing to you because I'm told you have many talented barbers in North Carolina; though I've not been there in many years, word of their skill has reached me here. If there is anyone in your fair town, possessing such skills and willing to relocate, please reply to me by letter or telegram at your earliest chance. Yours in Christ, Bishop.'"

It was all Octavius could do to remain seated. *This is it. This is the divine guidance I've been waiting for.*

"If anyone is interested in the position or knows someone who might be, please see me after service." Sister Brownlee folded the letter and continued on with the rest of the announcements.

He found it difficult to pay much attention to the rest of the events and happenings, he was too busy reeling inside. For nearly six months, he'd been scouring out-of-state newspapers, sending telegrams to far flung associates, and gathering as much information as he could, in order to make a decision on where he and Missy should move. Now, it seemed the answer had come, directly from heaven.

Missy, barely awake now as her exhaustion got the better of her, leaned her head against his shoulder. He cradled her close and did his best to follow the rest of service. Within the hour, he, his wife, and the other parishioners were flowing through the church's front doors, greeting the rector as they departed. He paused in the vestibule, long enough to converse with Sister Brownlee and ask that she forward his information to the Reverend Sims when she replied to his letter on Rector Billups' behalf.

Outside, the sun shone brightly in a cloudless blue sky, belying the chill lingering in the air. Missy leaned against him heavily, and he took care as he helped her onto the seat of their buggy. Climbing in beside her, he wrapped her woolen cloak close around her body, then added the blanket he kept under the seat; to assure she was warm on the short drive home. "You're still feeling poorly, my love."

She nodded, her face lined with tiredness. "I hope I've shown the Lord my devotion...I feel like death. If I take to my bed now, I may have hope of feeling better by Christmas."

"It's still two weeks away," he commented as he popped the reigns and got their mare underway. "I'll have Doc Trent visit you again tomorrow, and whatever he directs, I'll take care of it."

"Bless you, husband." She let her head fall against his shoulder again, and closed her eyes.

Smiling, he drove his wife home.

-Abraham-

January 1893
Edenton, NC

Grasping the looped handle of his cowhide portfolio, Abraham Jackson stopped in front of the quaint, plank exterior of a one-story building facing the corner of King and

Broad Streets. Silently, he assessed the hand painted sign above the swinging doors.

Lipsey's Store and Bar Room.

His brother John finally caught up then, and nearly strode right past him, until he stuck out his forearm to block his progress. "Tap your brakes, brother. This is the place."

John glanced at the sign for a moment before his gaze shifted. "Sorry, I was…er…distracted."

He glanced further down King Street and caught sight of a shapely woman in a deep blue traveling costume, moving away from them at a steady pace. Rolling his eyes, he elbowed John. "Get your mind on the matters at hand, brother, and off the local ladies."

Appearing a bit chastised, John tugged the lapels of his coat. "Pardon me, but you must admit, she was quite the specimen."

He shook his head and sighed. "I'll admit no such thing. Now get your tailfeathers inside, Mr. Williams is probably in there waiting for us." He pushed open one of the doors and moved inside, with his brother close behind.

Inside the establishment, he admired the hand-carved pine bar and nodded to the apron clad man behind it. The space hosted a good-sized crowd of men of all races, seated at the round pine tables scattered around the large room. Beyond this communal space, where fellows were engaged in eating, drinking, card-playing and manly conversation, a second door stood open on the back wall, with another sign above it that read: Goods and Sundries.

Abe approached the bar and gestured to the barkeep. "Afternoon, sir."

The man, a round older gentleman with a ready smile and a bearded jaw, touched the brim of his cap. "Welcome in. Name's Lipsey, and this here's my place. What'll you have?"

"Two apple ciders, and a bit of information, if you don't mind." Abe reached into his pocket and handed the man a half-eagle.

Lipsey nodded and added the money to his cash box. As he produced two mugs and placed short sticks of cinnamon in each, he said, "What do you need to know?"

"We're looking for Mr. Octavius Williams."

Lipsey filled their ciders from one of the taps, then slid their drinks toward them. Pointing, he said, "That's him, over at the corner table by the piano."

"Thank you." Abe and his brother both took their drinks, and they made their way over the sawdust floor toward the lone man the barkeep had pointed out.

Williams stood as they approached. Clean shaven and dressed in a blue shirt, denims, and boots, he appeared a little older than them, but still relatively young. He stuck out his hand as they came to the table. "You're the Johnson brothers, right?"

Abe nodded, offering a smile as he shook his hand. "Yes, Mr. Williams. I'm Abraham, and this is my younger brother John. We're pleased to finally meet you, sir."

He chuckled. "Likewise. Call me Octavius, no need to be so formal."

"Fair play, then. You can call me Abe."

They sat down; Abe in the middle with his brother to his left and Octavius to his right. After a quick sip of cider, he said, "Let's get to it; we don't want to monopolize too much of your time." He paused, remembering the information he'd been given about the Williamses. "Is your wife well, Mr.—er, I mean, Octavius?"

"As well as can be expected. Missouri is with child and has been quite weak and sickly." His subtle smile communicated his deep love for her. "I try not to add to her concerns, so I'm making this a personal undertaking."

"Good man," John commented. "I'm sure she appreciates you showing such care."

"Agreed. We'll keep this brief, so you don't have to be away from the missus too long." Setting the portfolio on the table, Abe extracted the papers. "I'll begin with a little about us. John and I are Houston-born, and we're both pursuing our education at The Howard Institute."

"Wonderful." Octavius appeared genuinely pleased. "What are you studying?"

"I'm a first-year chemical sciences student," John replied. "And my brother is in his last year of studying business and economics."

"Impressive...you two must be quite intelligent." Octavius shrugged. "Your pursuits sound far more complex than barbering, I'd say."

"Maybe so, but we respect tradesmen and laborers of all types." Abe located the maps he'd been looking for, and placed them in the center of the table. "My brother and I are also interested in civic and community work, which is our role today. We're here on behalf of our benefactors, Mr. Thomas Waggaman, Mr. Charles Bane, and Reverend John Sims, as well as the twenty-three members of our association, the Capitol Brotherhood, to facilitate your move to Washington D.C. and the purchase of the rowhouse located at 338 U St. NW in LeDroit Park."

Octavius moved his chair closer to the table and leaned in. "Alright. Tell me more about this whole enterprise."

John cleared his throat then, and delivered his well-practiced speech. "The Capitol Brotherhood is a collective of men of color of all backgrounds, who mainly come from Anacostia and Howardtown. While Mr. Waggaman and Mr. Bane are white, their investments in real estate, as well as their stance as folks who embrace the ideals of fairness and equality, are their motivations in funding us. Our goals are civil service, community uplift, and equality in education and access to resources. We advocate for the full, speedy integration of the nation's capital, and our current focus is LeDroit Park, where we see great opportunity for property ownership for Black families in particular."

"Right," Abe added, picking up his part. The Capitol Brotherhood offers support and protection from supremacists and other miscreants, and it has collected funds for down payments, furniture, and other necessities. We've already started the process with three other Black families who will be moving to LeDroit ."

"So, my wife and I won't be the only Black family, then." Octavius propped his elbows on the table.

"No," John shook his head. "But we're not sure who will be the first. Right now, it's a question of whose sale will go through the quickest. We can say that Mr. Gregory, the owner of the U St. NW home is very motivated to unload the property."

"Our benefactors tell us that Mr. Gregory is divorceé from Colorado." Abe slid the home's floorplan toward Octavius. "He needs to return home to Colorado Spring right away to look after his ailing father, and doesn't much care about the background of the buyer."

"I see." Octavius took the diagram, and gathered a few of the maps as well. "Let me look these things over." He appeared contemplative as he perused the information, including the diagram of the home's layout, maps of the LeDroit Park and of Washington D.C., and a list of resources the Brotherhood had compiled to share with the families they were working with.

When he thought enough time had elapsed, Abe asked, "Questions?"

"What's this list?" Octavius held up the paper.

"Those are all the businesses and establishments in town

that are owned by Brotherhood members and associates, or by people of color." Abe had helped compile the list as part of an assignment for his Collective Economics class and was quite proud of it. "Part of our work necessitates the recirculation of our money within our communities, so we're encouraging our families to support these good folks."

"There's a bit of everything there," John added before draining the rest of his cider. "Grocers, hairdressers, eateries. There's even a medical section; and we can recommend Mrs. Anderson's midwifery skills- she teaches at Howard."

Octavius nodded. "Stellar—my wife and I will be needing her services."

"You can keep all those papers, we've plenty of duplicates." Abe passed Octavius a large tan envelope. "Use this to keep everything together."

"So, what are your thoughts so far?" John tented his fingers, awaiting an answer.

"I feel pretty sound in my decision to make this move," Octavius said, scratching his chin. "I'm wondering, though. What does this protection offered by the Brotherhood look like?"

"Simple. We don't know how the white residents of LeDroit will react to your presence, but we anticipate not everyone will be welcoming. The men in our group will rotate night watch duties at your home, per your request, should you feel it's necessary." Abe tucked his remaining papers away. "There's no cost to your family for this, and the ten men who make up the guard group are all armed, trained in firearm safety, and comfortable with good old-fashioned brawling."

His brow furrowing, a smile tipped Octavius' lips. "Are you a part of the guard group, Abe?"

"He's not, but I am," John grinned. "And I'm at your service."

Octavius stood then, extending his hand. "I must say, I feel very confident in what we're doing. Count me and my wife in."

Abe rose to his feet, accepting the offered handshake. "Magnificent. We'll be in touch to get you prepared for the sale and the move."

CHAPTER 5

-Octavius-

May 1893
Raleigh, NC

Hoisting one of his wife's large trunks off the ground, Octavius passed it to the waiting porter, who tucked the trunk into the open door of the baggage car. A twinge shot through his back, and he stood to his full height and reached above his head, hoping to stretch the area a bit. *My back will surely pay the price for this later.*

Raleigh's train station was larger than any station closer to Edenton, and boasted a far greater number of available trains and destinations. The station had a plank platform extending along the rear of the large, red-brick building. Tall steel posts supported the tin roof overhead, and glass paned windows provided a view of the cherry benches and polished floors inside. Wider metal columns marked the boundary of the platform, where it dipped to the ground before giving way to the tracks. The station and platform area were alive with the activity of passengers, railroad employees, and all manner of folks. The air, already thick with early summer humidity, smelled of coal and smoke.

"My, my," Sweety commented as he dragged yet another, slightly smaller trunk off the back of his buggy and eased it onto the plank platform. "You all certainly have a lot of things."

"It's mostly Missouri's; I think she owns enough skirts and dresses to clothe a small village," Octavius joked. "And this is only some of it; she left a few things at mother's house this morning." For a moment, he recalled his earlier conversation with his mother, father-in-law, and grandmother. Grandma Milly had offered a sleepy smile and a peck on his cheek from the comfort of her bed, while his mother and Dorsey had given Octavius and Missouri hearty hugs and words of goodbye. He could clearly remember the tears standing in his mother's eyes when they'd left. *Mother smiled through it, bless her. Still, I know she's sad.*

Sweety chuckled then, breaking through the hazy barrier of Octavius' thoughts. "Yes, women tend to collect a lot, but I've found it's best to let them have it. After all, a good wife makes an easy life."

"That's the truth." He glanced across the platform at his wife, who stood off to the side with his sister Jo. Seven months pregnant, Missouri was radiant with new life, and his heart swelled as he watched her circle her palm slowly over her large, rounded belly. *The Lord has finally seen fit to bless us with a baby, and I mean to give both my wife and my child the very best life I can.*

He and Sweety assisted the porter in getting the last of their luggage onto the baggage.

Watching his wife and sister, he saw them talking, but was too far away to hear their words among the noise and commotion happening around him. He smiled as Jo draped her arms around Missouri and hugged her. Their sisterly bond was clear, and part of him truly regretted having to separate the two of them.

The train that would take his small family to the District of Columbia disgorged a load of passengers, and he watched the people spill out to cross the platform with their bags in hand. Some folks began to line up at the ticket window, while others headed for the window where a woman was selling sandwiches and lemonade to travelers. Others took seats on the low wooden benches to get their bearings.

A whistle blew, and Octavius watched as the porters slid the doors of the baggage cars closed, securing their cargo for the journey ahead.

A railroad conductor standing on the platform proclaimed, "Calling all Passengers for Richmond, Washington D.C., and points north!"

He walked over to where his wife and sister stood with Sweety close behind him.

"We've loaded everything," Sweety said, his attention on Missouri.

"Yep. We can board now, sweetheart." Octavius draped his arm around his wife's waist, enjoying her serene answering smile.

The atmosphere grew somber for a moment, and no one spoke. The four of them simply gazed at each other, as if each of them was committing the others' features to memory. He felt an uncharacteristic sense of melancholy, and he sighed as the weight of it gripped him, tightening his chest.

Missouri grasped Josephine's hand, clutching it within her own. "Until we meet again, Jo."

"Safe travels, Missouri." Josephine captured her for another tight hug, leaving just enough space between them to accommodate Missy's belly.

As Missouri stepped back, Octavius moved closer to his

sister. "You have watched over me since I was no taller than a blade of grass. You have talked me down from many a high tree limb, and I don't know what I will do without you."

She smiled through her tears. "You won't have to do without me. I'll be pestering you by letter and visiting as often as I can."

He chuckled, even as he felt the moisture gathering in his eyes. "I will miss you, sister. Keep yourself well."

"I will. You do the same, brother. Promise to send a telegram so we'll know you arrived safely."

"I promise." He hugged her, and whispered, "I love you, Josephine."

"I love you, too." Jo's wavering voice gave away her emotions as she spoke.

Inside of him, sadness and uncertainty did battle with excitement and determination. It was all he could do to clear his throat and straighten his posture as all the thoughts tumbling around in his head fought for supremacy.

Releasing Jo, he returned to his wife's side and began guiding her toward the train. Knowing that her changing body made her a bit unsure on her feet, he kept a steadying hand on the small of her back so she wouldn't stumble as the stepped off the platform and onto the car the conductor indicated. Letting the task claim his full attention kept him from looking back at the loving family he'd be leaving behind.

The inside of the Jim Crow car, located behind the baggage cars, could only be described as ordinary. Sturdy wooden benches lined each side of the central aisle, while short muslin curtains hung on the sides of each glass paned window. Many of the seats were already filled with Black travelers, barred from sitting in the fancier cars with white passengers. Guiding Missouri gently toward an empty bench, he helped her get settled and then sat down next to her.

Glancing out the window, he offered a wave to Jo and Sweety, who were still standing on the platform.

The shrill sound of the train whistle filled the air, the engine huffing and puffing clouds of steam and ash. Placing his arm around his wife's shoulders, Octavius kept his eyes fixed on his sister's tear-stained face until he could no longer see her.

-Missouri-

As the steam engine chugged down the track, taking them further from the comforts of home with each passing moments, Missouri stared out of the window, watching the scenery roll by. The sun hung low in the sky, illuminating the pastoral green woodlands surrounding the tracks.

It's beautiful countryside...I'd probably be enjoying it if I felt better.

She shifted about on the unforgiving wooden bench beneath her hips, but try as she might, she couldn't seem to find a comfortable position. Her large belly left very little space between it and the seat in front of them, and she didn't want to trouble the passengers in front of them by constantly bumping their seat back. So, she settled into a spot, tamping down her rising discomfort as best she could, while longing for the softness of her settee back in their place back in Edenton.

She sighed at the thought. *Guess that little cabin's not really ours anymore.*

Octavius' voice broke through her thoughts then. "What's troubling you, my love?"

"It'd be faster to tell you what isn't troubling me," she

lamented, letting her head drop against the steady strength of his shoulder.

"Oh, my poor darling." He draped his arm around her upper back and cradled her close to him. "Tell me all about it... we've plenty of time before the next stop."

"Where are we, anyway?" Despite the brutality of the stiff seat, she'd dozed off earlier, and had missed some of the trip.

"We're somewhere between Rocky Mount and Richmond," he answered. "I believe we crossed over the border into Virginia a while ago." Giving her a squeeze, he said, "Now, go on and tell me why you're upset, Missy."

She inhaled deeply, then blew the breath out. "Well, to begin with, sitting on this hard bench feels like sitting on a boulder. I'm already so stiff, it will be a wonder if I can get up when we do stop."

He snapped his fingers then, as if remembering something. "Goodness, I can't believe I forgot." Releasing his hold on her, he bent low, sliding his satchel out from beneath the seat.

She watched as he opened the bag and began rifling through the contents. "What are you doing?"

"Just a minute." He continued his rummaging, then suddenly stopped. "Aha. There it is." Righting himself in the seat, he presented her with two items: a small stuffed pillow shaped like a cylinder, and an even smaller sealed tin. "Grandma sent them along for you, gave them to me this morning."

"Bless her." She slipped the pillow behind the small of her back, leaned against it, and groaned with delight as a good deal of the pressure she'd felt there dissipated. "This pillow may be magic."

He shrugged. "Maybe. She said she'd added some kind of herbs to the stuffing..."

"Oh!" The rollicking motion of the train, as it rounded a

curve in the track, jostled her a bit in her seat. Righting herself again, she said, "Do go on."

"But the real magic is in the tin, according to Grandma."

She opened the tin then, peering at the semi-solid substance inside, which was speckled with what looked like dried herbs, or perhaps flowers. She raised it to her nose and sniffed. "It smells like cloves. What is it?"

"Salve. I'm to rub some on your sore places, to ease the pain." He winked, dropping his voice to a whisper. "I'll rub the places that aren't sore, as well."

She elbowed him gently. "Oh, go on with you. That's how I got in this predicament." She cradled her belly, circling her palms over it. "I'm glad Milly was so thoughtful to send these things."

"Me too; it means I can fix at least one thing that's troubling my sweet love." He pecked her on the cheek. "Tell me the other things, and let's see what we can do about them."

"I'm already missing home and family, of course." She leaned against him again, welcoming his embrace. "Then, I've so many worries about what life in D.C. will be like...not just for us, but for our baby."

He was silent for a few moments, and seemed to be pondering what she'd said. "Sounds like you're afraid."

"I am," she admitted. "At least a little."

He cleared his throat. "Well, wife, that makes two of us."

She inclined her head so she could look into the dark umber eyes that had stolen her heart many moons ago. "You mean that?"

He nodded. "I sure do. I don't know anyone who wouldn't be nervous about such a move; anyone who says he isn't is likely to be lying, far as I'm concerned."

That gave her a measure of comfort. "I reckon we'll just be afraid together, then." She shifted her gaze back toward the passing scenery, which was becoming harder to see as sunset melted into dusk. "Between my achy joints, the baby kicking me and jumping up and down on my innards, and all these feelings tumbling around inside me...I declare, I'm fit to be tied."

His answering chuckle was soft. "It's alright, baby doll. Anybody would be at sixes and sevens, considering all the changes we're making right now. I don't know that I can fix how you feel, but let me ask you something."

She turned her attention back toward him, and that handsome face she loved so well. "What's the question, husband?"

His tone and his expression serious, he asked, "Do you trust me, Missouri?"

"Yes." She answered without hesitation. "Of course I do, I trust you with my very life."

He smiled. "Good. I made the decision to go North, and you put up no resistance. I think we both know its best, even if it is a bit uncomfortable for the time being." He placed curved fingers beneath her chin, settling his gaze on her face. "You are the most precious thing in my life, and I'd do anything, and I do mean anything, to keep you safe and see you happy. And if that means I have to do it scared, then so be it."

For the umpteenth time today, she felt the tears gathering in her eyes only a moment before they began sliding down her cheeks. "You're such a charmer, 'Tavi."

"I meant every word."

"I know." She leaned in and kissed him on the lips. "I love you."

"I love you, too."

The conductor passed through the car then, announcing in a loud voice, "We're due in Richmond in about half an hour, and we'll stop there and deboard for some brief maintenance."

"Good," she whispered to her husband. "Hopefully I can make it to Richmond before my bladder bursts. The baby has been doing somersaults for the past little while." In the dim light, she could make out the outline of a tiny elbow or foot, moving just beneath the surface of her skin.

Laughing, he held her close and lay his large palm against her belly. "This baby is going to be a pistol...I just know it."

CHAPTER 6

Night was deep as the train rolled into the station at Fredericksburg, Virginia, the last stop before Washington, the sound of the squealing brakes and the high-pitched wail of the whistle awakening Octavius from a somewhat restless slumber. The car's interior lights had been turned down hours ago, and as he glanced outside, only the lamps hanging from the poles at the station helped beat back the encroaching darkness.

The elder Mexican couple who'd been seated in front of them waved as they departed, taking their valises with them.

"Viaje seguro, amigo," the man said to Octavius. "Safe journey, my friend."

"To you, as well." He nodded to them as they went on their way, shifting his gaze briefly to the empty bench they'd left behind. *I wonder if the conductor would let Missouri stretch out on that seat?*

Next to him, his wife was asleep. Her head had fallen against the windowpane, and her snores were soft and rhythmic. It did him good to see her at rest, even in such an awkward setting and position.

I'll rub her down good once we arrive...make sure she won't be too stiff.

The train rocked slightly from side to side with the motion of passengers walking and luggage being shifted about, and he watched the goings on from his perch on the seat. The conductor had informed them back in Richmond that they'd only be at the Fredericksburg station long enough to release deboarding passengers and pick up those who'd be joining them, so he didn't bother getting up.

We're almost there...just a few more hours. He raked his open palm over his face, then stifled a yawn.

His eye was drawn to the pair of passengers who appeared in the doorway, then moved toward the seat the elder couple had just vacated. A stout, older Black woman, dressed in a simple dark skirt and white shirt, wore a small flowered hat over the black curls that framed her round face. She clutched the hand of a young man who exceeded her in height by quite a few inches, dressed in denims, a tan shirt, and worn boots. The young man carried two good sized bags in his free hand, and his tight expression communicated either worry, distaste, or both.

As the pair slipped into the forward seat, Octavius put aside his notion of having his wife stretch out there. He was repositioning himself in the seat, as the wheels of the train began spinning again, when the lady in the flowered hat spoke. "Evening, Mister." She kept her voice low, likely out of courtesy to the passengers who were sleeping.

He met her gaze in the dim light, matching her volume. "Evening, ma'am."

"Name's Cora Lee." She stuck out her hand. "Pleased to meet you."

He shook her hand, taking note of her simple and

forward nature. "I'm Octavius." He inclined his head toward Missy. "That's my wife, Missouri."

Cora Lee grinned. "Oh, she's about to pop, bless her soul. She sure is pretty."

He smiled. "That's very kind of you. If she were awake, I'm sure she'd be obliged." Gesturing to the rather sullen looking young man, he asked, "Who's your traveling companion?"

She pursed her lips, but only for a moment. "Pardon my sour puss, honey. That's my great-nephew, Albert." She poked him in the forearm with her index finger. "For heaven's sake, Albert. Speak to the man."

Without turning around, the youngster groused, "Hello."

Shaking her head, Cora Lee sighed. "That boy's head is as hard as a rock, always has been. Anyway, he's seventeen, so I supposed that's to be expected."

Octavius chuckled. "I'd wager my mother had similar problems with me at that age." He'd lived thirty-five years thus far, but he was certain his mother had wanted to throttle him at least once or twice in the days of his youth.

"Where you and your pretty wife headed to?" Cora Lee asked, turning her body in her seat as if to get a better look at them.

"Washington, D.C."

"Visiting someone?"

He shook his head. "Going to live there, raise our baby."

Cora Lee smiled. "Going off to start a new life, then? Amen." She appeared thoughtful for a few moments and quiet settled between them. When she spoke again, her tone had lowered to a near-whisper. "We're starting over, too, me and Albert."

The boy grumbled something, but Octavius couldn't make it out. Rather than inquiring as to what might have been said, he asked, "Are you headed to D.C. as well?"

Cora Lee shook her head. "Nope. We'll be on this steam bucket clear on to New York. My daughter and son-in-law live up there, and we'll be moving in with them."

"You two are from Fredericksburg?"

"No, sir. We from a lil' place called Locust Grove. It's a good twenty miles or more west of the "burg.""

What's got them boarding a train in the dark of night, heading so far north? Octavius felt his brow furrow, but he had a pretty solid feeling there was no need to pose the question out loud. *If I wait, she'll tell me the story.*

Sure enough, as the sun rose and the passengers, including Missy, began to stir, Cora Lee cleared her throat. "It's quite a tale that landed us on this train, you know."

Octavius straightened in his seat, keeping one arm around his groggy, but aware wife.

"What's going on?" Missy asked in a sleep heavy voice, rubbing her eyes.

"Well, baby doll, this is Miss Cora Lee and her grand-nephew Albert. They got on in Fredericksburg, and now she's gonna say why they're headed for New York."

"Nice to meet you, honey," Cora Lee offered.

"Likewise," Missy replied.

"Well," Cora Lee began. "You see, my great-nephew has taken a shine to Miss Hannah, the son of a mill owner back home. Now, I suppose that would have been alright, even though that family's above our station and all. But you see, the problem comes in 'cause Miss Hannah and her people is *white*." She emphasized the last word.

Albert, who appeared only half-awake in his seat, grumbled again, but contributed nothing further.

Missy cringed. "Oh, Lord."

"Oh, Lord is right," Cora Lee quipped. "That gal's father wasn't none too pleased to see them making eyes at each other, and he made it clear Albert wasn't to even speak to her. But you know how young folks are...they set they mind on somebody, claim they in love, and you can't hardly do nothing to keep 'em apart." She sighed. "So, his mama, my niece, asked me to get him outta town. And here we be."

Octavius shook his head. "Life in the south is just too much to bear at times."

They chatted more about their experiences, and Octavius even shared the occurrences at last year's Juneteenth celebration. "That's when I decided, we had to go north."

Cora Lee nodded. "You've done endured enough. We all have."

Albert, who'd kept his own counsel up to that point, finally spoke. "I... suppose we're doing right by going to New York then, auntie." He paused. "Even if...I never do see Hannah again."

"You better believe it, child." Cora Lee squeezed her nephew's shoulder. "And you'll forget that gal before you know it."

-Missouri-

May 1893
Washington, D.C.

With an old shirt tied around her head to keep her hair out of her face, Missouri sat on the tile floor in her new kitchen. The crate next to her had been filled with their dishes and cooking pots, which she worked to arrange in a manner so that they'd all fit in the lower cabinets. She'd donned a stained shirt, and a pair of trousers her husband no longer wore, to avoid ruining any of her good clothes while attending to the work ahead.

They'd been in their new place, a rowhouse at 338 U Street Northwest, for six days. Looking around at the many crates that remained to be addressed, she blew out a breath. *Goodness. It may take us until Christmas to get settled...I just want to do as much as possible before the baby comes.* To that end, she leaned her upper body into the cabinet and began arranging the things she'd tucked inside.

She heard the shuffling of feet as Octavius entered the room. "How goes it, my love?"

Extracting her head from the cabinet, she looked up at him, taking in his attire: a faded union suit and a pair of worn-down moccasins. "I'm mostly finished...just looking for a creative way to get everything to fit."

He chuckled. "I don't know if it's the number of things we have, or the size of the cabinets that's the problem."

She glanced back into the cabinet's dark interior, seeing the precariously placed stacks of items within. "May be a bit of both. Whatever the case, I've done the best I can to make it work."

"Well, I did manage to fit all my clothes into my designated side of the wardrobe upstairs," he said as he approached her and leaned down. Placing a kiss atop her head, he straightened again. "What will you assign me to do next?"

Shutting the cabinet, she quipped, "Help me up off of this floor. There's no way I can lift this hefty belly on my own."

He extended his hands, and she grabbed them. He gave a firm, but gentle tug that lifted her from the floor. Just as she got to her feet, the doorbell chimed.

"Hmmm. I wasn't expecting any callers," he remarked.

"Neither was I... heck, we don't know anybody yet."

She followed her husband through the dining room and into the front parlor, hanging back a bit as he approached the door.

"Who is it?" he asked, hand resting on the bronze doorknob.

"Hello, Mr. Williams," a male voice called from the other side of the door. "It's me, Abraham Jackson."

She relaxed a bit, recognizing the name of the young man who'd facilitated their purchase of the house.

Octavius turned the knob. "Come on in, Abe. What brings you here?"

Abe, dressed in a blue shirt, brown trousers, and a brown bowler, crossed the threshold. "I just wanted to see how you and the missus are adjusting to life here in the Capitol. Are you two settling in?"

"We're alright," Octavius replied. "Still unpacking and arranging things."

"That stands to reason...after all, it's only been a week." Abe paused, and seemed to notice her for the first time. Snatching off his hat, he held it against his chest. "Good afternoon, Mrs. Williams. I beg your finest pardon."

She smiled, amused and entertained by his fancy manner of speech. "It's alright, Abe. I was lurking here in the corner after all. Welcome to our home."

"Thank you kindly, ma'am." Abe replaced his bowler. "It's high time we had a fine, upstanding couple like yourselves in LeDroit Park. Yes, sir, high time. Is there anything you need from me? Any way I can assist?"

Octavius laughed. "Don't tempt my wife; she won't hesitate to put you to work."

She grinned. "There actually is one thing we could use your help with." She inclined her head, gesturing toward the upright piano they'd haphazardly placed in the dining room. "Do you think you and my husband can move my piano?"

Abe rubbed his hands together. "Certainly. Where would you like it?"

She pointed above. "Upstairs, in the spare bedroom on the second floor."

Abe cringed. "That will take a bit of effort...but we'll handle it."

"Don't say I didn't warn you, Abe," Octavius said with another chuckle, and led the young man to the dining room to retrieve the instrument.

Feeling the exhaustion of the day's labor catching up with her, she moved to the settee beneath the window and took a seat. The ligaments in her hips were pulsing like a drum beat, and the pain was beginning to radiate into her thighs and buttocks. As she reclined against the back of the settee, she grazed her hand over her belly. The baby seemed to respond, and she watched as the fabric of her shirt puckered and undulated in time with her belly as the little one changed position inside her.

The men were huffing and puffing their way slowly up the stairs, with Abe walking backwards with one end of the piano and Octavius on the other end.

As they reached the first landing, a loud CRACK sliced through the air.

She bolted upright in her seat. "What was that?"

Before anyone could answer her, the sound came again, louder and closer. This time, it was accompanied by the distinctive sound of it impacting a solid surface. She slowly glanced over her shoulder. *Did something just hit the outside of the house?*

Octavius dropped the piano, diving toward her as he screamed, "Missy, get down!"

She did as he instructed, sliding her hips off the settee and onto the hardwood floor in a single quick motion, and he was upon her before she could draw her next breath.

She couldn't see past her husband, but she heard the echoing thud of the piano hitting the floor and the bump-thump-bump of it sliding back down the stairs. *Lord, is Abe alright?* She knew better than to try and extract herself from

Octavius' tight, protective hold as he pinned her to the floor.

The cracking sounds continued, coming faster and closer together. Soon a cacophony rose to accompany the hellish cracking: the shrill shattering of glass, the impact and splintering of wood, and a strange thrumming she couldn't identify. Her heart pounded rapidly, and the baby turned somersaults inside her, as if aware of the goings-on. Overwhelmed, she squeezed her eyes shut against the horror of it all.

Finally, mercifully, the sound ceased, and the house grew quiet. She spent a long time with her eyes closed, listening to the sounds of her own shaky breaths, as well as her husband's.

"I... think they've gone now." Abe's voice, low and somber, emanated from somewhere in the room.

Grateful to hear his voice, she opened her eyes. Staring up at her husband, she found his concerned gaze waiting.

"Are you alright, my love?"

She nodded. "I suppose. I mean, I'm not hurt."

He shifted then, allowing her a bit of space and helping her sit upright again.

She glanced around, and saw the piano resting awkwardly on its side at the foot of the stairs, the music rack broken and the lid dangling. There was a line on the floor where the piano's feet had scratched the wood, and some of the trinkets she'd placed on the mantle had also toppled over in the fracas. Despite all the things she saw, she didn't see their visitor. "Abe? Where are you?"

"Here." He sat up then, and she could see he'd been lying on his back on the landing between the two flights of stairs. As she viewed him between the staircase slats, he snatched a handkerchief from his pocket and mopped his brow. "Praise the Lord, I'm here."

Octavius climbed to his feet, and she noted the palpable aura of panic and anger he exuded. Marching over to the front door, he flung it open again and stepped outside.

She wanted to follow him, but couldn't get to her feet alone. So, she waited, while Abe stood and made his way back down the stairs toward the fallen piano.

Octavius burst back inside, holding a slat of wood in his hand. "There's bullets lodged in the bricks out there," he shouted, without directing his words at anyone in particular. "And I found this nonsense on the front steps." He turned the slat of wood around, so they could see it.

Abe folded his arms over his chest. "What in Sam Hill?" He and Octavius exchange a pointed look, as if passing a message between them.

She gasped as she read the words crudely scrawled on the board, in large red letters.

NIGGERS GO HOME.

Her entire body trembled as hot tears filled her eyes, spilling down her cheeks.

When he saw her crying, Octavius shut the door and tossed the board aside. Kneeling on the floor beside her, he drew her into his arms.

"We've traveled all this way... to be... safe," she muttered between sobs. "Why...would someone...do this?"

"I'll keep you safe, Missy," he vowed, pressing her close to him. "I'll guard you with my life."

CHAPTER 7

-Octavius-

August 1893
Washington, DC

Octavius reported to the Capitol building on a warm, sunny August morning, with his barbering tools and important documents in hand. According to the correspondence he'd received, he was to interview with the Senate Sergeant at Arms, a Mr. Richard J. Bright, to secure the position at the congressional barber shop. Nearly 5 weeks had passed since Bishop Sims' retirement, and Octavius imagined there'd be quite a backlog of requests after such an extended period.

If I'm right about the approach I've chosen, I'll most certainly get the job.

With a wife and infant daughter at home to support, he was about as motivated in his pursuit of the position as a man could be.

He'd taken one of the city's impressive electric-powered

streetcars from the stop at Rhode Island Avenue NW and 6th Street NW, which had whisked him south and west toward the Capitol. The journey allowed him a comfortable trip and a chance to view some of the city.

After getting off at 1st and B Streets, he navigated the grand, well-maintained grounds to find the entrance. The interior, cavernous and overstated in every way, had lustrous polished marble floors, stone walls inlaid with arches and carvings, and bronze statuary celebrating famous statesmen. To the right of the center point of the huge room, a uniformed guard seated behind a desk rose when Octavius appeared. "What's your business here, boy?"

The man's words echoed in the expansive space. Drawing a breath and tamping down his true opinion about being called 'boy,' Octavius produced the correspondence he'd received from the Sergeant at Arms. "I have an appointment with the honorable Mr. Bright."

The guard reviewed the paper for a few moments, then passed it back. "Go straight down this corridor, then turn left. The office will be the second door on your right."

"Thank you." Octavius returned the paper to its spot inside his bag and headed in the direction indicated. Arriving at the interior office, which had a painted marker with Mr. Bright's name and position on the small window set in the door, he met with a young woman in a tan ensemble only slightly darker than her pale skin tone, seated at a desk in the outer office.

"Good morning. Mr. Williams, I assume?" the woman trilled as he approached her.

"Yes, ma'am."

She pointed to her right. "You can go on in, Mr. Bright is waiting."

He offered his thanks and proceeded, still marveling at

the architecture and furnishings surrounding him, as well as the generally subdued atmosphere.

Before he could knock on the door, it swung open, and a white man of average height appeared, with a flat mop of brown hair that turned gray around the sideburns, and a thick brown mustache obscuring his upper lip. "Williams! Good man, you're right on time. Come in."

"Good afternoon, Mr. Bright." He entered, taking a seat before the rather imposing desk as his host indicated with a gesture, placing the bag with his tools and important documents on his lap.

Bright took his seat behind the desk, leaning back in the big leather chair. "I've had many candidates for this position, Mr. Williams. But only one applicant had a personal referral from the Bishop, our beloved former barber. And that's why you're here today."

"Yes, sir. I appreciate the Bishop's faith in me." He'd only briefly met the old minister, in a gathering orchestrated by the Johnson brothers, a few days after they'd arrived in town. Their conversation had apparently provided Bishop with enough assurance in his skill to make such a recommendation. "How do assessments for the position usually go?"

"Well, I've already looked over your documents, so I know who you are, where you've come from, and where you've worked." Bright stroked his mustache. "I'd say the next step is for me to see you perform the duties you'll be handling as our barber."

"I've brought my instruments." He patted his bag.

"Excellent. We'll proceed to the basement, where the barbershop is, momentarily." Bright paused. "Before we do, I need to make you aware of the run of things here."

"Of course, sir."

Clearing his throat, Bright announced, "My position as

Sergeant at Arms means that I'm the doorkeeper, the intermediary...the last line of defense, if you will, between this nation's lawmakers and anyone who might have ill intent toward them. I'm responsible for their safety, but also, for their needs being met, so they can do their jobs. Understand?"

"Yes, I do."

"Good. So, I'll be making my decision based on the sacred duties I uphold." He straightened his dark tie. "No one else has ever had this position, left it, and returned, so I also have my reputation to be concerned with."

"Ah, yes," Octavius said. "I do recall reading that you previously served in this office...between '79 and '83, if memory serves."

Bright's brown eyes narrowed slightly, and his mustache twitched. "I see you've done your diligence, then."

"I try to be as informed as I can, sir." Octavius had long since come to understand the value of knowing what he was walking into, of arming himself with as much knowledge as possible, and of a bit of flattery where needed.

"I like that." A smile tipped the mustached lips, but it disappeared almost as quickly as it came. "Follow me, and let's see what you can do."

Following Bright through what seemed like a maze of marble corridors and staircases, they arrived at the thick wooden door marked "Capitol Barbershop." The room, larger than Bright's office, but nowhere near as huge as the rotunda upstairs, offered adequate space for a long counter with two barber stations, as well as a small waiting area with a bench for clients to await their turn in the leather barber chairs.

Bright moved immediately to the first chair and took a seat. " I could use a bit of tidying on top, and maybe a slight trim of the mustache. Careful not to take off too much."

"No problem, Mr. Bright." Taking a moment to set up his tools and implements, which he preferred over the fancy implements laid out on the counter, he first draped the sergeant with a linen cape to protect his tailored, expensive looking dark suit from any fallen hair or products.

With that done, he proceeded to trim Bright's hair and mustache. Using a bit of the orange oil preparation his sister had taught him to make, he smoothed it through the hair to make it a bit easier to comb through. Then, he used his personal shears to trim away the shaggy ends and excess growth.

When he was done, he used his fluffy horsehair brush to dust off any specks of hair from Bright's neck and shoulders, then removed the cape with a flourish. Handing Bright the ornate brass hand mirror on the counter, he asked, "How is that, sir?"

After a few moments of silently regarding his reflection, Bright grinned. "Well, I'll be. Looks pretty darn good...the missus is bound to be pleased."

"I'm glad you like it." Octavius began cleaning and putting away his tools, as he'd become accustomed to doing over many years of barbering. He carried a bottle of Jo's cleansing mixture in his barbering bag, as well as a soft cloth, for such purposes.

Bright stood, and offered his hand. "I'll be glad to have you as our barber, Mr. Williams. That is, if you can start tomorrow, at nine o'clock, sharp."

Tucking away the shears he'd just wiped, Octavius shook Bright's hand. "Thank you, sir. I'll be here."

"Good man. I'll have my secretary draw up your agreement, and get you an official badge and uniform. Yes, we'll sort out all that tomorrow." Bright headed for the door. "Think you can find your way out?"

He nodded. "I think so. Thank you again."

"Welcome aboard, Williams." Offering a crisp salute,

Bright opened the shop door and disappeared down the corridor.

Alone in the room, Octavius beamed as he packed away the last of his implements.

I've got to get home and tell Missy...I know she'll be delighted.

-Missouri-

"Just hold the door for me, husband. I've got it."

With their one-month-old resting in the crook of one arm, and her handbag in her free hand, Missouri moved through the front door and into her parlor, grateful to escape the humid air flowing over the Potomac. Fortunately, the interior of the house was noticeable cooler.

Octavius entered behind her, shutting and locking their door. "Good Lord, it's hot out there."

"As Hades," she replied. "I thought we'd escaped such weather by coming up here."

He shook his head. "I suppose not. Maybe we should have gone farther north."

"I think not." She laughed as she made her way across the room. "We're plenty far from home, if you ask me."

He closed one of the drapes over the front window, dampening the glow of sunlight streaming into the room, something he did on warm days to keep the temperature down. "You're amazing, my love. Only a few weeks into motherhood, and you've taken to it beautifully."

Lowering herself slowly onto the settee, careful to avoid jostling their daughter or her own still-healing body, she smiled at her husband. "I'm glad you noticed." Sitting her purse on the cushion, she shifted baby Vivian so that her tiny head rested against her shoulder. The baby released an audible breath as she changed position.

"How could I not?" He picked up her handbag and hung it

on the coat rack, then joined her on the settee. "I feel like one wandering in the wilderness, still trying to figure her out. Meanwhile, you seem to know what she needs before she does."

Bouncing the baby gently against her body, she chuckled. "I don't have any special powers, honey. And you're no rube with her...you're doing just fine as a father."

Vivian fussed then, releasing series of high-pitched whines.

Hastily, she lay Vivian across her lap and undid the top four buttons of her blouse. "Help me, honey."

Octavius assisted with undoing the cloth strip she'd used to bind herself, as her body couldn't yet abide by corsets. Vivian uttered a single plaintive wail, but before the babe could begin crying in earnest, Missy had freed her breasts, and she deftly lifted the baby to one so she could suckle.

He scooted closer to her, draping his arm around her shoulders.

She glanced his way, and while he said nothing, his soft smile and the light in his eyes spoke to her, communicating his love for her, and for their daughter.

They settled into comfortable silence while Vivian nursed, content to share in the awe and wonder of their life together. When the baby had her fill of mother's milk, she handed her over to Octavius. "Now, help her belch, like I showed you."

He lay the baby on her belly over his lap, and gave her back a few gentle taps. "Like this?"

Vivian's tiny belch answered before Missy did.

"As I said, you're a fine father." She kissed his cheek, lifting her daughter into her arms again. Seeing her drowsy appearance, and her miniscule fists rubbing at her eyes, she smiled knowingly. "Take her upstairs and put her in the bassinet; she'll soon be asleep."

She watched as her husband dutifully ferried the baby upstairs, grateful for his presence and his love.

When he returned, he reclaimed his place next to her on the settee. "It was nice of Bishop to invite us to service at Universal Holiness, wasn't it?"

She nodded. "It was. I enjoyed his sermon, and the singing, and getting to meet some of the people from around here." She paused, looking at the old clock in the corner by the staircase. "Goodness. I'd better start the coffee...the Greenbriars will be here before long."

Octavius stood. "What can I do to help, my love?"

She tapped her chin, thinking. "It's too warm to sit on the veranda, so set the table in the dining room. And open the window in there to let some air circulate."

"I'll take care of it." He left the room a moment later.

She passed though the dining room and went into the kitchen in the back of the house. There, she put on a fresh pot of coffee and removed the large stoneware dish containing her peach cobbler from the icebox. Firing the stove, she set the dish inside to allow the cobbler to heat up, so it would be warm when the time came to serve it.

Within the hour, she and her husband sat in the dining room with the three members of the Greenbriar family. The second Black family to move into LeDroit Park, they were friendly and jovial, if still a bit nervous.

The Greenbriar matriarch, Agnes, forked up a piece of cobbler and consumed it with great delight. "My goodness, Missouri. You must give me you cobbler recipe—it's divine!"

"Thank you, Agnes. Just remind me and I'll copy it down for you before you leave." She smiled, genuinely enjoying the compliment. "That means a lot coming from you, since you're a baker."

"I call things as I see them, sugar." Agnes ate another bite before adding, "I don't plan on serving cobbler, ya know, if

I ever get my little bakery business set up here. But I certainly plan on eating plenty of it."

"Coffee's pretty good, too," added Martin, Agnes' husband. "Takes skill to make good coffee...a lot of folks don't know that."

Octavius laughed. "I'm a lucky man, my wife has many talents."

"You flatter me, husband." Turning toward fifteen-year-old Francine, the Greenbriar's lovely, yet reserved daughter, Missouri asked, "So, dear. What's your favorite subject in school?"

A small flicker of excitement lit her dark eyes. "Well, ma'am, I enjoy the sciences. The arithmetic is alright, sometimes. But science is my real favorite."

Missouri smiled. "That means you've got a head for figuring things out, solving problems. Good on you."

"You know, we probably wouldn't have uprooted from our place in Georgia and come all the way up here," Martin admitted. "But when the Brotherhood contacted us, we could see how it would work out alright."

"We figure, if we can get established, you know, get my bakery open and get Martin on the machinery staff at the Howard Institute, then our baby can go to school there." Agnes slid her empty plate toward the center of the table.

"What are your thoughts on that, Miss Francine?" Octavius asked.

She offered a shy smile. "That would be wonderful. I've been thinking of going there to study medicine."

"Nursing," Martin corrected.

"I think she said it right," Agnes countered, giving her daughter's shoulder a squeeze.

"In the meantime," Francine offered. "I could look after your little one, when you need me. That way I could maybe save a few dollars toward my tuition."

Missouri nodded. "That would be lovely." As much as she adored her baby, there were moments of deep exhaustion or overwhelming busyness that beset her at times. "I'll be sure and call on you when we need a little respite, then."

After the Greenbriars departed and afternoon waned into evening, Missouri saw to Vivian's changing and feeding, then tucked the baby into the small woven basket she favored as a portable bassinet, resting it on the table while she chopped carrots for dinner. She and Octavius enjoyed a dinner of roast chicken, honeyed carrots and mashed potatoes.

John arrived for his shift of night watch shortly after dinner, with his pistol on the hip of his denims.

"Would you like some chicken, John?" Missouri offered their guest, who'd become more like a nephew to them.

John shook his head as he moved to his usual spot on the settee. "I already ate, Mrs. Williams. Thank you, though."

Though the night guards rarely accepted, she always offered food. The Brotherhood never charged them anything for protecting the house; she felt feeding the young men was the least she could do to show her appreciation.

Later, in the darkness, she lay next to her husband, who was still reading a copy of *The Evening Star* by lamplight. To her left, Vivian slumbered in her bassinet next to their bed. "I'm tired, honey. I'm going to sleep."

"I'll lower my lamp, then." He did so, then leaned over to peck her on the cheek.

CHAPTER 8

-Octavius-

Thud.
Rattle.
Clang.

ctavius' eyes popped open, though he saw nothing but blackness. The strange series of sounds he'd heard had jarred him from his sleep. Without hesitation, he got to his feet and blinked a few times, allowing his vision to adjust to the inky darkness. Then he moved silently toward the bedroom window, which looked out onto U Street. Drawing back the curtain and peering out, he saw a shadowy figure in the moonlight, near the front of the house. The refuse bin was overturned, and the mysterious figure hunched over it, holding something in his hand.

Is that...could that be...a gun? Not one to take chances when it came to the safety of his family, he roused Missouri with a firm, but gentle shake.

She opened her eyes, looked at him. "Darling? What is it?"

In a harsh whisper he replied, "Get the baby, and get on the floor."

Another clang sounded outside. Hurriedly, Missy got up, grabbed Vivian, and cradled her as she shrank into the corner between the wardrobe and the wall.

Seeing his wife and child in such a position angered him, but he had no time to deal with that now. "Don't move, my love. Stay here until I come back."

She nodded vigorously.

Jamming his feet into his moccasins, he grabbed the rifle he kept next to his nightstand and tipped downstairs. He found John on the settee looking out the living room window. Inclining his head toward the window, John looked at him and held up three fingers.

So, there are three of them.

No sooner than Octavius could join John by the window, the shots began. A series of loud cracks shattered the calm of night. Both men fell to the floor, and a moment later, the front window over the settee shattered.

Bullets continued to whiz by as they regrouped.

John hastily wrapped a piece of the curtain around his fist and knocked away the broken glass around the edge of the window frame. Both men returned fire then; John from his Laumann automatic pistol and Octavius from his trusty Winchester Model 1891.

A male voice hollered, "Damn it, I'm out!" and a there was break in the shots.

Crouched low between the settee and the armchair, Octavius could see the three men near the western edge of his property, fumbling around with their munitions. Seizing the opportunity, he lined up his shot, aided by the moonlight and the glow cast by the street lamps, and plugged one of them in the leg.

A scream pierced the air, and one man went down hard,

like a sack of grain. The other two men began shouting at one another, before hoisting up their fallen comrade trying to run off down the street.

John jumped up, and Octavius was close behind. Swinging open his front door, Octavius followed the men up U Street, with the butt of his rifle in hand and the business end resting against his shoulder.

Their progress was slowed significantly by their injured friend, so he didn't need to run; he simply took long steps. John and his pistol were behind him the whole way. At the corner of U and 3rd, the injured man slipped from the grasp of the other two, forcing them to pause and regroup.

Octavius handed his rifle over to John. "Trade."

"Sure thing." John passed him the pistol.

When the exchange was made, Octavius marched up to the three miscreants who'd harassed his family and disturbed his sleep. *They do this on a Monday morning no less, after we've had such a lovely day with our neighbors.*

In a few hours, he be at the barber shop, and he hoped to heaven he'd have his wits about him to do his job properly after this rude interruption of his rest.

While John trained the rifle on the men, Octavius announced, "Hands up, jackasses."

All three men stopped, and six hands were lifted in the air. The injured man, now seated on the ground looking forlorn, seemed to be struggling to keep his hands raised.

They were all young, by the look of things. One of the men, narrow as a fencepost, stood trembling on the outer edge of the walk. His bare face seemed more the result of youth than of shaving. The one who'd taken the shot had a bandana tied around the lower half of his face, but his bright blond curls peeking from beneath a bowler made him appear young.

Approaching to the bigger of the three, who stood to the

right of the one with the hole in his leg, Octavius silently assessed him for a moment. His round face, shaggy brown beard, and cold blue eyes were not nearly as impressive the man likely assumed them to be.

For a moment, he considered the absurdity of the situation. *These three idiots may not be old enough to know any better, but somebody thought it wise to send them to terrorize my family.*

Whatever the case, he had a message to relay, and he meant to have it clearly understood and delivered to the responsible party. Resting the pistol muzzle against the fat man's temple, Octavius spoke, venom dripping from every word. "Go and tell whatever asshole that sent you to my house, that we shoot back. And next time, we shoot to kill. Now, get a move on."

He and John kept their guns aimed and watched as the men gathered themselves as best they could, then scurried away up 3rd Street. Once the men were gone, Octavius and John trudged back to the house.

John stopped in the living room as he shut and locked the door. "Any boards or old wood around here? We're gonna need to patch that window, 'til you can get the pane replaced."

Not wanting to think about what that would cost, Octavius replied, "There's some plywood in that little closet on the veranda. It's right by the back door." He headed up the stairs as he spoke, and he could hear the baby fussing as he approached.

Back in his bedroom, he found a terrified looking Missy, still dutifully tucked into the corner with Vivian in her arms.

"Octavius! Thank God you're safe." Tears gathered in her eyes.

He knelt, gathering them both close to him. "I'm sorry about this, honey."

"It's not your fault. " Missy leaned heavily against him. "Thank you for protecting us."

"It's my most sacred duty, my love." He kissed her brow, noting the moisture gathered there.

"One I hope you don't need to take up again any time soon," Missy said.

Vivian continued to cry softly, and he could feel his daughter's small body contracting in time with her sobs. Missy broke away from his embrace briefly, and held the baby against her shoulder, making a shushing sound and rhythmically patting her bottom. "There, there, little one. Everything's alright. See? Father has returned."

Vivian's fussing tapered off, soon fading into deep breaths with a few exasperated coos sprinkled in.

Looking at the two of them, the most precious things in his whole world, Octavius let out a sigh, feeling as if he'd been holding his breath since he'd first been awakened by the ruckus beneath his window. He thought back on the fat man, and the expression of mixed fear and vitriol in those cold blue eyes.

I did what needed to be done. And for the sake of my family, I'll do much worse if I must.

-Missouri-

September 1893
Washington, D.C.

On a warm September evening, Missouri sat in one of the chairs at the small circular table on the veranda. The slick glass surface of the table reflected the multicolored tapestry of the sky above, as twilight approached. Her sweet baby, Vivian, lay across her lap, sleeping. Glancing down at her little one, Missouri stroked her soft curls, careful not to jostle her.

The week had been an exciting one, with the arrival of her sister-in-law Josephine on her first visit to their home. Jo had described her train journey from North Carolina as smooth and mostly uneventful, but she'd also hinted that things back home were in something of an uproar. Over the last few days, she'd revealed bits and pieces of the tale, and she seemed to be unsure of what her next course of action would be.

Knowing Jo, she'll make the right choice. She's got the best head for business of anybody I know.

Turning her attention to her much-loved guest, who sat next to her nursing a cup of hot tea, she remarked, "You're awfully quiet, Jo. What's on your mind?"

She released a long sigh. "I'm still thinking on what I will do with my lot in Cheapside."

Nodding, Missy said, "You've been here for a week, and that is all you've talked about."

Jo cringed. "I know. I'm sorry. Is there something else you wish me to discuss?"

"I'd like to know that my nieces and all the family back home in Edenton are doing all right." Missy offered a chuckle. "If that's not too much trouble."

She shook her head, then cleared her throat. "Let's see. Sweety is doing well and spending more and more time at the barbershop since he never hired a replacement for Octavius. Clara has taken a teaching job in Littleton, as is doing well as of her last correspondence. Florrie has finished her courses at the Badham School and is looking to start foreign language studies at Bennett College next fall."

Missy smiled as she heard all the good things happening to her kin. "Wonderful. And how are Jeannette, Dorsey, and your grandmother Milly getting on?"

"Mama and Dorsey are good. She's still gardening, he's still building houses. I don't suppose he'll ever retire; he loves it too much. And Grandma, well, she doesn't get around as well as she once did, but she's still got her wits about her. I go over there once a week to play chess with her."

"And how does that go?"

"She beats the pants off me most of the time, but the conversation is so good, I keep crawling back for another clobbering."

Missy laughed out loud at that admission. *So, there's one thing Jo has yet to master, then.*

Vivian stirred, and Missy realized her amusement had probably woken her. The baby opened her eyes, rubbing them with her tiny fists as she began to cry, voicing her disapproval at being disturbed. She adjusted her shirt and let the babe latch on to nurse. "All right, all right. Now that I've heard about that, let's work on your problem."

Octavius walked out of the house then, a tumbler of lemonade in hand, and took a seat in the empty chair next to his wife. "Yes, let's talk about this Cheapside conundrum. It won't do to have you wandering around my home with such a long face, sister."

Jo turned in her chair, looking back and forth between the faces of her brother and sister-in-law, her expression one of trepidation. "I must decide whether to sell the lot or to rebuild. And I must make my decision before I return home to Edenton. I just can't bear to anguish over it any longer."

Missy, rocking the baby side to side, nodded her head. "I can see how hard this must have been on you. You simply haven't been yourself. I've missed you so, and I hoped your first visit to our home would be a happier one."

"So did I," Octavius added. "I also hoped you'd bring the family with you, rather than taking the train all this way by yourself."

"I know, I know. Sweety can't get away from the shop for any length of time until he hires on another barber or two, and Florrie has gone to Littleton to visit with Clara." Jo wrung her hands, rubbing them against one another. "I promise I'll bring them the next time I visit."

"Deal." Octavius pointed to his sister's journal. "Could you tear a sheet of paper out of your book for me, please? And hand me that pencil."

Jo complied, ripping the last sheet from the book, and handing over the page, and a pencil along with it.

Curious as to what her husband would do, Missy leaned closer to him to observe his actions.

He laid the paper down on the table, and drew a line down the center, creating two columns. At the top of one column, he wrote the word SELL in large letters, then underlined it. He wrote the word REBUILD at the top of the other column and underlined that as well. "Now, my method isn't exactly scientific, but it does depend on logic."

"All right," Jo said. "Do you think I haven't been thinking logically up until now?"

He shook his head. "No, you haven't. You can't, because your emotions are so tied into this. I can tell by the way you've been carrying on."

"How's that?" Jo tilted her head, her eyes narrowing just enough to be perceived.

Watching the two of them, Missy couldn't shake her sense of fascination. It seemed like the roles in their sibling relationship were being reversed.

"Pacing the floor, talking to yourself. Picking at your food." He shook his head. "Your whole mind is occupied with your property and what to do next. But in order to make the best decision, you have to look at this situation logically." He tapped the pencil on the paper. "We're going to weigh the benefits of selling against the benefits of rebuilding, and that's how we'll decide."

Jo blinked several times in succession, her shock plain. "Heavens, Octavius. You're making good sense."

"Of course I am, and don't look so surprised about it!" He released a short burst of laughter. "Come now, let's start with our list. Tell me one good thing that will happen if you sell that old lot."

"Well, I'd get an infusion of cash from the sale."

"All right, cash is always good," he replied while jotting the word "cash" on the paper. "Name something else."

While Missy split her attention between their conversation, and keeping baby Vivian content, they continued their discussion until they collected four reasons Jo should sell: money, freedom from maintaining the property, giving someone else a chance to build there, and the ability to move on to something else.

Having noted all that, he asked his sister. "Now we move on to reasons to rebuild. Go on, rattle them off and I'll take them down."

Jo tapped her chin. "I'd get a fresh start, I'd keep my property portfolio intact, I'd infuse money into the local economy by hiring carpenters and craftsmen..."

"Dadgum, Jo, slow down! I can only write so fast."

Jo giggled, paused a few moments so he could catch up, then started up again. "The new building would be my own design, not just something I bought. I could increase the overall value of my holdings, I'd be participating in the revitalization of an important historic district, and I—"

Missy, having heard enough, held up her hand. "Jo, stop."

A puzzled looking Jo asked, "What is it?"

"Do you hear yourself? Do you hear the way you sound, dashing off all the reasons to rebuild?"

"I . . . suppose I hadn't thought about that. How many reasons do I have now, Octavius?"

"Four to sell, and six to rebuild." He winked. "The numbers don't lie, sister dear."

Jo released a long, slow exhale, as if she'd been holding her breath for a long time. "There's one more reason, and I think it might be the best reason of all."

"What's that?" Missy asked.

"Clara and Florrie." Her voice shook with emotion as she spoke. "This is my chance to teach them a life lesson by example. To show them that when life destroys our dreams, we can begin anew, better than before."

Missy wiped away a tear that suddenly streaked down her face. "Well, Jo, I believe you've made your decision."

Jo clasped her hands together, her lips tilting into a smile. "Yes. And it's all thanks to my favorite dunderhead."

Octavius grinned. "Anytime, Jo. Anytime."

"I've one more favor to ask. Send a telegram to Hannibal Badham for me and ask him to recommend the best iron-work builder he knows."

Octavius rose from the table in short order. "Certainly. I'll take a hack to the telegraph office now."

As Missy watched, Jo began furiously writing in her journal, what appeared to be directions and specifications for the rebuilding of her property. She smiled to herself as she lifted Vivian onto her shoulder to burp her.

I think she's getting fired up about it. Yes, Jo will be just fine.

CHAPTER 9

-Octavius-

4 March 1897
Washington, D.C.

Octavius joined the throngs of people moving across the Capitol grounds toward the Senate wing, careful to maintain his grip on Vivian's tiny hand. Missouri walked alongside, holding their daughter's other hand. They'd found this method of travel by foot especially effective in both keeping up with their little one, whose curiosity often caused her to wander off. It also allowed them to steady her tiny, somewhat wobbly steps, while keeping pace with her parents' much longer strides.

The day was sunny, but it couldn't be called warm; the temperature hovered only a few degrees above freezing. The late morning light bathed the lush green grounds and illuminated the mass of people around him. They were all from different walks of life, different races and creeds, but a historic event had united them in this place today: the inauguration of William McKinley as the 25th president of the United States. They navigated the rows of chairs that had positioned in the grass, facing the flag-festooned dais where the ceremony would take place. Octavius' position as an employee of the Capitol afforded them seats only a few rows from the front, and once they'd settled into their chairs, he looked around at some of the familiar faces. He saw many of the lawmakers he served, including Mr. Pearson, the representative from North Carolina's 9th district, who'd become a regular at the shop once he realized he and Octavius were from the same home state. A few seats down and two rows ahead sat Senate Minority Leader Arthur P. Gorman, a Maryland Democrat with a gruff personality and a rather stubborn cowlick.

"Did you get to groom the president-elect for his big moment?" Missouri asked, as she used a handkerchief to wipe a mystery smudge from Vivian's jaw.

He shook his head. "No, he and Mr. Hobart have their own private barbers. But I did work on most of the lawmakers here, and yesterday, I worked on Justice Miller." He gestured to the tallish fellow sitting on the dais in his judiciary robe, who would soon perform his duty as Chief Justice in administering the oath of office to McKinley.

Soon, all the chairs were filled in, and a crowd of onlookers had gathered beyond the designated seating area, standing shoulder to shoulder as the event opened with a brief welcome and prayer. A representative of the Bishops of the African Methodist Episcopal Church rose from his seat on the dais, and announced the presentation of the Bible upon which McKinley would swear his oath. He held up the book for everyone to see. "We have marked an important verse for the president-elect, II Chronicles 1:10, which reads thusly: *Give me now wisdom and knowledge, that I may go out and come in before this people: for who can judge this thy people, that is so great?"* With that said, the minister handed the Bible over to Justice Miller. As outgoing president Cleveland, clad in long overcoat and satin top hat, looked on, McKinley lay his hand on the book and took the oath.

Once Mr. Hobart had been administered his vice-presidential oath, those in attendance prepared for McKinley's inaugural address. Vivian, seated between her parents, squirmed in her chair. One look at his daughter let Octavius know she was getting antsy. *She's only four.... her capacity for sitting still is limited.* "Are you alright, Vivi? Do you need to use the facilities?"

"No, Papa." She shook her head, the ribbon draped curls bouncing in time with the motion. "I want to play..." she whined.

"Oh, baby. I know you're tired of sitting," Missouri said softly as she tucked a lock of hair behind Vivian's ear. "But this is an important day. We must be very good and very quiet until the speeches are finished, alright?"

"Yes, Momma." Settled, at least for the moment, she wiggled her bottom until her back rested against the chair again, letting her legs dangle over the edge of the seat.

She gave her a peck on the cheek. "Good girl." Brushing off this minor distraction, Octavius returned his attention to the historic happenings in front of him, and tuned in to McKinley's remarks.

"The national verdict of 1896 has for the most part been executed. Whatever remains unfulfilled is a continuing obligation resting with undiminished force upon the Executive and the Congress. But fortunate as our condition is, its permanence can only be assured by sound business methods and strict economy in national administration and legislation. We should not permit our great prosperity to lead us to reckless ventures in business or profligacy in public expenditures. "

Octavius shook his head, leaning toward his wife. "That's such an obvious dig at old Jennings Bryan and his proselytizing behalf of silver."

She giggled. "Clearly. But what is politics without a bit of pettiness and competition?"

"Pretty dull, I'd wager." He chuckled to himself.

The speech wore on, and Octavius remembered all the news and chatter leading up to the election. Aside from McKinley and Bryan's feuding over whether gold or silver should be used for currency, the two men had demonstrated vastly different strategies while campaigning for the vote. Bryan had traveled the country, making grand speeches about currency reform; while McKinley had remained at home in Canton, Ohio, where he gave his well-honed pitch from his front porch.

Mckinley's tone changed, as if he were about to point out something of great importance. "If there are those among us who would make our way more difficult, we must not be disheartened, but the more earnestly dedicate ourselves to the task upon which we have rightly entered. The path of progress is seldom smooth. New things are often found hard to do. Our fathers found them so. We find them so. They are inconvenient. They cost us something. But are we not made better for the effort and sacrifice, and are not those we serve lifted up and blessed?"

"I wonder if he means to make real change for folks who look like us, and not just folks who look like him," Missy commented.

"Let's hope he's going to do right by us." Octavius grabbed his wife's hand and gave it a small squeeze.

McKinley fixed the crowd with a penetrating stare. "We will be consoled, too, with the fact that opposition has confronted every onward movement of the Republic from its opening hour until now, but without success. The Republic has marched on and on, and its step has exalted freedom and humanity. We are undergoing the same ordeal as did our predecessors nearly a century ago. We are following the course they blazed. They triumphed. Will their successors falter and plead organic impotency in the nation?"

When the ceremony ended, and the crowd began to disburse, Octavius rose from his chair and lifted Vivian into his arms, then placed her on his shoulders. "You must have to go tinkle by now, Vivi."

She nodded. "Yes, Papa. Where is it?"

He looked around, and saw the guard standing by the service entrance to the Senate wing. "I'll take you over here, it's near where Papa works."

He weaved his way through the tangle of people, with his daughter perched on his shoulders and his wife holding his hand. At the door, the guard initially offered him a stern look, before breaking into a smile. "How are you, Williams? This the wife and daughter?"

"Yep, this is my little family," Octavius commented. "Say, Vic. You think we could sneak in here so Vivi can use the facilities?"

"Sure thing." The man stepped aside, and they entered the building.

Missouri stared around, her eyes wide with awe, as they moved down the corridor. "Goodness. I've never seen so much marble in all my days."

"This is just the basement. You should see how much stone and gilding they've used upstairs," Octavius said as he opened the door to the john.

"I'll go in with her," Missouri said.

He placed Vivian on the floor, and watched as she grabbed her mother's hand and the two of them disappeared into the small room. After a few minutes, they returned.

"Let me show you where I work," he whispered, gesturing

them to follow. A short while later, he used his key to unlock the barber shop door, and swung it open.

Missouri went to the counter, admiring the polished brass instruments. "These tools are mighty fancy."

"You're right about that." He laughed. "I never use them; I prefer my own."

Vivian got loose from her mother, and took the opportunity to climb up on the bench in the waiting area, her little moccasins marring the cushion with blades of grass and dust. "It's bouncy!"

Missouri grabbed her and placed her back on the floor. "Vivi! No jumping on the furniture."

Vivian's lower lip poked out, and tears gathered in her eyes as she tucked her hands behind her, tugging at the big bow tied around the waist of her pink dress.

With a shake of his head, he grabbed a clean cloth and doused it with a bit of cleaning solution. Stooping down, he handed it to his forlorn looking child. "Vivi, go over there, and clean where you got the seat dirty."

She sniffled, but accepted the cloth and dutifully wiped away the traces of her youthful exuberance. The task took some effort on her part, but she kept at it.

"Good job, sweetheart." He took the cloth and tossed it into the bin under his station.

"Didn't you say you had tickets to the inaugural luncheon?" Missouri asked.

He nodded. "Yes, but with Vivi along, I'd just as soon return home and leave the rest of this pageantry to the politicians."

She came into his personal space, and placed a soft kiss on his cheek. "Yes, husband. Let's take our baby home."

-Missouri-

June 1900
Washington, D.C.

"Come now, Vivi. You're holding us up."

Missouri stood outside her daughter's door, resting her hands on her hips, as she watched her snatch every piece of clothing she owned from her dresser drawers. Each item that wasn't what the child wanted landed unceremoniously on the floor, and both the growing pile and the ticking clock were starting to raise Missouri's ire.

"Mama, I want to wear my red ribbon! Teacher says it's one of the colors of Africa." At seven, Vivian already displayed great intelligence and curiosity; one never knew what she might say.

"But dearest, your white ribbon goes with everything." Missouri held up the hair ornament she'd been clutching.

Vivian ceased her searching, the characteristic pout on her face. "It's not the same, Mama."

"I know. But if we don't get across to the Dunbar's house soon, we'll miss the party." Missouri felt the presence of someone behind her, and before she could turn, she heard a familiar voice.

"Somebody need a red ribbon in here?" Florrie appeared in the hallway, holding not one, but two of the much-desired hair ribbons. Tall and slender at twenty, she was a far cry from the chubby little girl who used to climb trees back home in Edenton.

Missouri blew out a breath. "Praise the Lord." *I'm so glad Florrie decided to summer here between semesters at teacher's college...Vivi has become such a handful.*

"I'll get her ready, auntie." Florrie eased past her and into Vivian's room. "So, do you want one puff, or two, cousin?"

Vivian squealed, grabbing Florrie's hand and tugging her toward the bed. "Let's make two puffs!"

Look at her. She'll do amazing with her students. "Please, make it quick." With a laugh, Missouri left her daughter in her niece's capable hands, and went in search of her husband. She found him in the bedroom, checking himself in the mirror. He looked handsome and casual in his denim trousers, short sleeved blue shirt, and black loafers.

"You look ready. That makes two of us," she quipped, walking behind him and draping her arms around his waist.

"Vivi still going mad about that ribbon?"

She shook her head. "Florrie's got two of them. We may make the party yet."

Together, they headed downstairs to await their niece and daughter, and once they were all assembled, they took the short walk up the road to the Dunbar home.

The brick rowhouse at 321 U Street NW was of similar construction to their own, though the layout on this side of the road had been slightly altered to allow wider homes. Mounting the short staircase that led to the porch, Missouri raised her hand to knock.

A moment later, the lady of the house opened the door. "Welcome, Williams family. So glad you could make it."

"We're much obliged, Mrs. Dunbar." Missouri said, the words escaping in a breathless rush. She saw Mrs. Dunbar tending her flowers in the small yard fronting the house, or passed her in the shops in the city. This was her first up-close look at the woman she considered a literary genius.

"Pshaw...call me Alice, honey." Slim and of petite stature, she wore a simple white blouse with a lace collar, and a tan skirt. Her hair was up in a topknot of sorts, while her gold earbobs and the cameo encircling her neck added a touch of glamour. With a raised hand, she gestured them inside. "We were going to do this on the terrace, but it's so powerfully hot. Anyway, make yourself at home, there's plenty food and drink in the kitchen."

As the four of them followed her into the house, Missouri did her best to keep her wits about her, and to keep an eye on Vivian's whereabouts.

"I'll look after Vivi," Florrie whispered, as if aware of her aunt's thoughts.

"Have I told you you're my favorite niece?" Missouri tapped the tip of Florrie's nose.

She laughed. "No, not as I recall. I promise to rub Clara's nose in it the minute I get home." Holding Vivian's hand, Florrie wove her way toward the kitchen.

Octavius, who'd been behind her since they entered, tapped her shoulder. "I see Judge Terrell over there...I'll just be paying my respects, my love." He pecked her on the cheek, and slipped away.

Standing in the Dunbar's front parlor, just a few feet away from where the Alice Dunbar held court, Missouri could feel the tremble rising within. Her inner voice chastised her not to go off the deep end and let her admiration make her look silly—or worse yet, make her hostess uncomfortable. *Don't gush, Missy. Don't embarrass this lady in her own house!*

The inner critic crowed on, but despite its edicts, she was only able to maintain her silent regard for a few more minutes before she blurted, "Mrs. Dunbar, I simply adored *Violets and Other Tales*!"

Their hostess, who'd had her back turned, paused her conversation and slowly revolved to face her. "My goodness, Dearie. Thank you for that!" She approached, taking both of Missouri's hands in her own. "Once again, though...call me Alice. There's no need to be so formal."

Missouri swallowed, drew a deep breath. "Pardon me, Mrs...er, I mean Alice. I'm just such a fan of your writing. I was able to get a copy of your latest...*The Goddess of St. Rocque* *and Other Stories...*and also your husbands *Poems of Cabin and Field.* I must say I enjoyed them both, but...your volume shows such a gift for nuanced storytelling, and..." Missouri stopped herself. "Excuse me, I shouldn't be rambling on, monopolizing you when you have guests."

Alice's smile, genuine and radiant, offered much comfort. "I can't say I ever tire of hearing how people have had positive interactions with my writing. Again, thank you for telling me that you liked it. Really, I appreciate your support." She released her hands. "Do you have your copy with you?"

Fishing around in her handbag, Missouri handed over the volume containing the Dunbar's joint effort. As she watched in awe, Alice retrieved a quill pen from the side table near her sofa, dipped it in the inkwell, and signed the title page with a flourish.

"There you are, dear." Alice replaced her pen. "If you want, I'll ask Paul to sign it as well."

On the verge of screaming, Missouri nodded, unable to form coherent words.

The gathering, well attended and lively, painted a picture of LeDroit Park that Missouri would have scarcely believed possible when she and her husband had moved there seven years prior. Not only had all the families assisted by the Brotherhood obtained homes there, but the area was becoming a place where the best and brightest of the Black community made their homes. Her subscription to the Evening Star kept her well-informed of the pertinent happenings for the city's Black citizens, and each day, she seemed to stumble upon a story of triumph and perseverance.

Rounding the corner from the kitchen into the dining room with a plate of food, Missouri saw the Terrell's seated side by side at the table, conversing quietly over their own food. Mr. Terrell, a lawyer by trade, now served as principle at the M Street High School, from which Francine Greenbriar graduated in '94. His wife, Mary, an Oberlin scholar and noted activist, served on the D.C. school board, something no other Black person had done before her.

I could pepper the two of them with a thousand questions...but I've embarrassed myself enough, I think. After greeting the couple and exchanging brief pleasantries, she set her mind on her food. Once she'd eaten, she returned to the kitchen to deposit her dish into the housemaid's bin. Glancing out the back window there, she saw Vivian running around the back yard with a few of the other young children of the neighborhood. The children were under the watchful eyes of the men seated on the terrace, namely Mr. Dunbar, Octavius, and the white-haired Sergeant Major Fleetwood. The highly respected veteran, who lived two doors down from the Dunbars, was decorated for his conduct during the war between the states.

Her gaze returned to Vivian, who was now being chased by Florrie; both girls appeared to be having great fun at their game. She smiled, unable to stop herself from thinking about that Juneteenth in Edenton back in '92, the fateful day that Octavius had decided they should make their home elsewhere. Who could have guessed that, eight years later, this sacred day set aside to celebrate freedom would turn out like this?

Octavius and I have a lovely home, our precious daughter, and a thriving community that has embraced us. It hasn't been easy, but it certainly has been worth it.

CHAPTER 10

-Octavius-

May 1910
Washington, D.C.

Untying his canvas apron, Octavius hung it on the small peg next to the barber station. He glanced around the shop, visually assuring himself that the place was neat and tidy, and would be ready for tomorrow's clientele. Noticing a dark smudge on the glass of the handheld mirror, he grabbed a linen cloth and dabbed on some cleaning solution.

What is that...hair dye, maybe?

He regarded his own reflection while scrubbing the mark off the glass. Fifty-two years of living had just begun to show, mainly in the slivers of gray in his mustache and sideburns. *Holding up pretty good, I think. All things considered.*

He set the mirror aside once he was satisfied with its cleanliness. Shrugging into his overcoat, he doused the lights and left the shop, using his key to lock the door behind him.

"Closing time, eh?" A familiar voice echoed behind him.

Turning, he smiled at Vic, the guard. The two of them had both been working in the Capitol building for over fifteen years, with Vic having started a few months after he did. "Sure enough, Vic. You headed home, too?"

Vic, brushing something off his dark blue uniform, shook his head. "I got another hour, then I'm gone." He held open the door at the end of the corridor, letting in the sound of softly falling rain.

"I'll see you tomorrow, Vic." Octavius set his brown bowler atop his head as he exited.

"Have a good evening." Vic waved, then closed himself inside.

Octavius crossed the grounds quickly, closing his coat against the raindrops pelting him. Heavy gray clouds hovered above, indicating that the rain would continue, and potentially, become heavier. He got himself to the streetcar stop as fast as he could, and waited under the small canopy there for only a few moments before he boarded the north bound car.

He arrived home within the hour, a bit damp but otherwise grateful. As he entered the house, shutting the door and hanging up his soggy coat and hat, he called out. "Missy? Vivi? I'm home."

His wife appeared in the dining room doorway. Wearing an apron over her brown housedress, she'd fashioned her hair into a low chignon, with a few silvery tendrils framing her lovely face.

Hmmm...never noticed that. When did she start getting gray?

A smile lit her face as she said, "Welcome home, husband."

He grinned, moving to where she stood so he could ease his arms around her waist. "Hello, my love." He kissed her softly on the lips. "Thirty years of marriage, and you haven't yet grown tired of me, eh?"

"Never." She cupped his jaw with her hand. "You're getting a bit shaggy...thinking of growing a beard?" Her tone was tinged with what sounded like excitement.

He thought about it for a moment. "Perhaps...if that's what my lady wants." He leaned low, placing soft kisses along the curve of her neck and collarbone.

Her responding giggles filled the room.

"Yuck," said a voice from somewhere behind him.

He extracted himself from the tempting, fragranced hollow of his wife's throat and turned his head. "Hello, Vivi."

Their daughter Vivian, just a few weeks shy of her seventeenth year, stood in the center of the parlor. Her arms were crossed over her chest, but she wore crooked half-smile. "Hi, Papa. Must you and Mama carry on like this?"

Missy quipped, "You ought to be glad...if it wasn't for such carrying on, you wouldn't be here."

Vivian blew out a breath. "Fair enough. But if you're both so keen on love and such, why won't you let me court, then?" She tilted her head, fixing them with a questioning stare.

He sighed. *This again. I suppose there will be no end to her complaints and queries until she gets her way.* His daughter was beautiful, her caramel skinned face bearing echoes of her mother, and of her late grandmother Jeanette. She'd grown tall over the last year or so, and had already exceeded Missy's height. Her long, dark hair, which she meticulously oiled and brushed, lay in thick waves around her shoulders, and she dressed and walked with the bearing of a sophisticated young woman. "Vivi, we've talked about this. You're a true beauty, and there's been no shortage of young men beating down our front door in hopes of winning your attention."

Vivian's smile brightened noticeably, and she grasped the end of her hair, twirling it around her finger. "Pshaw, Papa. You have an obligation to tell me I'm pretty."

"Maybe so, but that doesn't diminish how lovely you

are." He walked over to where she stood and pecked her on the forehead. "And what of those smitten young men? They can see your beauty just fine."

Missy chuckled. "They certainly can. Remember Rupert, who lives over on T Street by the Terrells? Showed up here three days in a row last week, clutching them flowers and asking after you."

That drew a rather pronounced eyeroll from Vivian. "Oh, Mama, Rupert's all knees and elbows. He's way too tall and skinny."

"He is mighty tall. Must be something to see on the basketball team." Missy shook her head. "What are they feeding that child?"

"He's not on the team, Mama. He's too clumsy and awkward...he's got no coordination to speak of."

Missy seemed poised to reply, but got so tickled that she couldn't speak through her laughter. When she recovered, she continued, "You really don't care for him, do you? That boy would gladly clean our floors with his tongue, if he thought you'd give him the time of day."

"Trust me, Mama," Vivian announced. "I'm interested in being courted, but NOT by Rupert."

She's got her eye on someone. Lord, I better sit down. Perched on the settee, he asked cautiously, "Well, if not Rupert, whom are you enamored with?"

Brown eyes sparkling, Vivian cooed, "*Armand.*"

Missy joined him on the settee, asking, "Who on earth is *Armand?*" She applied the same dramatic emphasis to the name as their daughter had.

Still standing, Vivian began to revolve slowly as she described the young man who'd captured her attention. "Oh, Mama. He's only about the smartest boy in my grade. Maybe even the smartest in all of M. Street High. He's an ace at arithmetic and science...he plays the violin...and he writes poetry." She paused as she whirled around to face them again. "And, his mother is from Brazil, so he can speak Spanish." She pressed her hand against her heart. "Oh, my heart flutters when I hear him speaking Spanish...the language is so romantic."

Regarding his starry-eyed daughter, he then looked to his wife. "Missy, what are we going to do with her?"

She shrugged. "I don't know. This Armand does sound pretty impressive, though. All that intelligence and speaking another language to boot."

He pursed his lips. "Now, Missy."

She laughed. "I'm just teasing you, honey. You say everything I want to hear and you only need one language to do it." Offering him a peck on the cheek, she said, "Will we adjust our edict about Vivi courting?"

He thought about it for few moments. "I suppose we'd better, before Armand the Magnificent is snatched up by some other girl."

Vivian, who seemed to have recovered from the spell she'd just been under, wedged herself between them on the settee. "I know you said I couldn't date until senior year. But that begins in August, just a few months from now. If you're willing to be flexible, I can enjoy some time with Armand this summer." She paused. "Supervised, chaperoned time, of course."

"Heavens, she makes a fair argument," Missy admitted.

"She does." He squeezed his daughter's shoulder. "You've shown us that you're a responsible young lady with good morals. Your school marks are good, and you don't give us too much trouble...beyond a bit of sass."

She had the decency to look ashamed, casting her gaze downward.

"I think we can give you this one concession," he continued. "But you need to finish the school year first, and maintain your marks. So, tell young Armand he can come around to see you after the term ends."

Falling onto him, she embraced him. "Thank you, Papa."

He held her for a moment, remembering the days when she was only a tot who fit comfortably on his lap. "You're welcome, Vivi."

Vivian extricated herself and got up, dashing for the stairs.

"Just remember," he called after her. "If any of these boys are disrespectful..."

Already upstairs, Vivian called back, "I know, Papa. You'll send them to Freedmen's Hospital on a gurney."

He smiled. *Just wanted be sure she hadn't forgotten.*

Next to him, Missy sighed. "Where has the time gone? Seems only yesterday she was just a baby...now she's nearly a woman."

Her words echoed how he felt inside. Embracing her, he pulled her close. "That's life, I suppose. Time is always ticking, while we're going through the motions of living."

"Well, I'm glad to be ticking my time with you." Missy brushed gentle fingertips over his jaw. "I love you, Octavius."

"Not near as much as I love you."

-Missouri-

December 1915
Edenton, NC

"I'm about ready for some dessert."

Hearing the disembodied male voice coming from her sister-in-law's front parlor, Missy moved across the kitchen, carefully cradling the dish holding her peach cobbler. She took slow steps as she navigated around butcher block, through the dining room and study to ferry the dish to the table that had been set up there.

The parlor of Josephine's house at 102 South Broad had been altered to accommodate the passel of family present for their Christmas feast. A few extra chairs had been moved into the room, and the settees had been positioned to provide additional seating in a central location.

She blew out a breath as she sat the dish down on the sideboard, alongside Josephine's cherry pie. She glanced at her daughter Vivian's first attempt at apple brown betty and wrinkled her nose. *Who knows? Maybe it'll taste better than it looks.*

The room was a bit cramped with all the bodies inside, but the sounds of laughter and easy conversation flowed all around her. She remained by the table as she looked over those in attendance, feeling her sentimentality rising.

The fireplace was lit, the flames roaring within casting a pleasant warmth throughout the space. The long garlands of pine and cranberries draped along the curtain rods and the mantel added a festive touch. The centerpiece, however, was the dwarf balsam tree, festooned with strung popcorn, carved wooden ornaments, and polished brass rings suspended on lengths of red ribbon. The thick fragrance of the needles mingled with the lingering smells of savory dishes they'd consumed, and the freshly brewed coffee that Clara had made to accompany dessert.

Jo's always been so stylish, in what she wears and how she keeps house.

Josephine, still the sister of her heart after so many years, sat on the far end of the flowered settee. Next to her, her eldest daughter Clara reclined; Clara's smartly dressed eighteen-year-old son Percy took up the end opposite his grandmother.

Missouri marveled at the sight. *I remember when Clara was*

just a little girl...here she is with a grown son. Never thought I'd be a great aunt.... but then again, never thought I'd be a grandmother, either.

She turned her attention to the other, solid brocade settee, where her twenty-two-year-old daughter sat. Next to Vivi sat her husband Harold Pelham, a recent graduate of the prestigious Lincoln University. Missouri watched, tears welling in her eyes, as Harry gently placed their infant daughter, Maurine, on his lap, while Vivian cooed sweetly at the baby.

Look at her. She couldn't be more precious...I well up every time I look at her. Maurine, a chubby little darling at six months old, had already captured the hearts of the entire family; but no one loved and doted on Maurine as much as her grand-parents.

In the midst of her emotional assessment of the present company, she realized her husband was missing from his seat in the old armchair. "Where's Octavius gotten to?" she asked.

"I think Uncle O went outside for a cigar," Clara volunteered.

"A cigar? It's freezing out there." Missy glanced toward the front window, and saw him standing on the porch, his back to her. "At least he's got his overcoat on." She would have preferred if he'd also donned his hat, which still hung on the coatrack. But after thirty-five years of marriage, she knew to pick her battles with her husband. Right now, she was content to enjoy this rare moment at home with the family she loved so dearly.

Josephine yawned, stretching her arms above her head. "I think I'll wait on my dessert. Right now, I want to hold my great niece." She started to get up, raising her hips a few inches, only to fall back against the cushions.

Percy stood. "Do you want me to fetch her, Grandma?"

Josephine shook her head. "No, Percy. I've got it." She rose slowly from her seat before shuffling across to where Vivian and Harold sat.

Missouri noted the way her sister-in-law moved, and felt the low hum of worry vibrating within. To her, Jo represented unmatched strength, determination, and intelligence. Goodness. *I hope she's alright... I can't stand to think she might be suffering.*

"Come here, my sweet baby." Josephine smiled as she gathered Maurine into her arms, then returned to her seat. Carefully lowering herself, she cradled the baby close and began humming to her.

The front door swung open then, and Octavius entered. "Cold out there," he huffed as he hung his coat on the rack, then eased back into his seat in Sweety's old armchair.

"Dessert, husband?" Missy asked. "Coffee?"

"No coffee." He waved his hand. "But I never turn down your cobbler, my love."

After fixing them both a helping, Missouri walked over and sat next to him in the kitchen chair she'd placed there earlier.

"So, Harry, what are you thinking of doing next, now that you've got your AB degree?" Percy, who now stood at the table sweetening his coffee, looked to his cousin-in-law with interest.

Harry, his arm draped around Vivian's shoulders, inclined his head. "Not sure yet. I've got a stable position in maintenance at the Capitol, thanks to my Papa-in-Law. Thinking about doing some post-graduate study at Howard...once we've saved our coins for tuition."

"Sounds solid," Percy replied as he sat down with his coffee. "It's the family trade for me, it seems."

"Barbering is in our blood," Josephine added. "Don't know if I'll ever put my shears down, myself. Though being in the shop these days is a bit melancholy...makes me think of my Sweety."

Missouri heard the pain in Jo's voice, and it rekindled her own mourning. She'd never forget those times; the final four years of the first decade of the new century had seen the family bury first Milly, then Sweety, then Jeanette and Dorsey.

As if sensing the direction of her thoughts, Octavius draped his arm around her shoulder. "Don't fret, Missy. Family love lasts always...even beyond this life."

The melancholy seemed to lift from Josephine, and she resumed humming and rocking the baby in her arms. "Such a beautiful baby. She's gonna be smart...I can tell."

Vivian laughed. "Big brains and big dreams run in this family, so I believe it."

"Big dreams, indeed," Clara added as she scooped up a slice of cherry pie. "I can't believe Florrie has gone down to Florida for the holiday instead of joining us; then again, she's always had her head in the clouds."

"That's my baby...Florence, the Adventurer," Josephine quipped.

Octavius piped up then. "We'll take Florrie to task when she returns, but it's no matter now. Look around this room. There are three generations of us here, right now." He made a sweeping gesture with his hand. "Jo and me, and our mother and grandmother before us, may they rest in peace, trudged through enslavement to make a better life. And this is the blessed result."

Missouri took in the faces of their loved ones, filled with the truth and power of her husband's words. Her own mother had falsified a report of her death when she was only a baby to secure her freedom, so she knew the ways enslavement had cast a lingering pain over their race.

"Great Uncle O is right," Percy declared. "This family is a force to be reckoned with and may we never forget it."

"Here, here." Harry raised his coffee cup in salute.

Positioning baby Maurine so that they faced each other, Josephine spoke softly to her. "Did you hear that, little one? You're going to be great someday. It's what this family does, no two ways about it."

Maurine yawned and stretched in response, a serene expression on her face.

"I believe we have an understanding," Josephine insisted.

Laughter erupted in the room then, and Missouri leaned into her husband's side as she joined in their shared amusement.

EPILOGUE

-Maurine-

17 March 1930
Washington, DC

*N*ow, *when did that come loose?*

Carefully retying the bow at her waist, Maurine adjusted the skirt of her yellow dress. In the half hour since the commencement of her grandparent's anniversary party, she felt as if she'd walked a hundred miles in trips between the kitchen and the front parlor alone.

She sighed as she checked her reflection in the mirror over the sink. *I thought I wanted to wear heels...now I'm glad Mama wouldn't let me.* Steeling herself for her return to fray, she opened the door to the second-floor bathroom and walked into the narrow hallway.

As she walked down the steps, her mother Vivian met her on the landing. "There you are, Maurine, I've been looking for you. We need—"

"Something from the kitchen?" She completed her mother's sentence with what she thought would come next.

Vivian's lips thinned, and she blinked a few times. "I declare, ever since you turned fourteen, you've become such a pistol."

"Sorry, Mama." Maurine's sheepish apology did little to soften her mother's ire, at least as far as she could tell. So, she added, "Have I told you how pretty you look today?"

Glancing down at her bronze satin frock, Vivian touched the cameo at her throat and smiled ever so slightly. "No... and lucky for you, I respond well to flattery." She reached out and gave her daughter's cheek a squeeze. "Now. Go out on the veranda, open the storage closet, and fetch two more bottles of wine for me, please."

"Yes, ma'am."

As her mother skittered down the stairs to rejoin the party, Maurine dutifully followed her to the first floor. Passing through the house, she went out the back door. After retrieving the two bottles her mother had requested, she brought them into the dining room and placed them in the big metal bucket of ice on the table.

Sidling up to her mother, she said quietly, "I've put the bottles on ice, Mama."

"Thank you, dearest." Vivian pecked her on the cheek before returning to her conversation.

Moving out of the way of the many guests scattered around the room, she went to the base of the stairs, where the old upright piano sat. Seated on the bench, she observed the happenings around her. Her gaze swung to her grandparents, who were seated side by side on the settee, holding court. Grandma Missy, with her white and gray curls surrounding her face like a halo, looked lovely in her gold brocade frock. Maurine knew from her mother's many announcements about the event that the dress had been custom made by a local Black seamstress for the occasion. Grandpa Octavius looked dapper in his dark suit, crisp white shirt, and bowtie. Maurine smiled when she saw the white satin handkerchief she'd given him as a gift, neatly folded into a diamond shape, positioned in his jacket pocket.

All around the couple were friends, neighbors, and admirers. Family was represented, too; cousin Percy had traveled all the way from North Carolina, and brought along his wife, Santoria. There were Black folks and white folks, along with some folks whose background Maurine couldn't guess. What she could see, though, was how well loved her grandparents were.

I wonder how Papa is faring in surgery? It's not every day he gets called to an emergency appendectomy. While she wished her father could have joined them at the party, she understood the importance of his work, and shared his interest in the complex inner workings of the human body.

Hearing the sound of silver striking glass, Maurine returned to reality. She saw her mother, tapping a tall, fancy glass with a fork. As everyone moved toward the center of the room, Maurine joined them, excusing herself as she wriggled through shoulder-to-shoulder bodies, seeking a spot from which she'd be able to see and hear.

Clearing her throat, Vivian lowered her glass and spoke. "I'd like to thank each of you for coming tonight, to celebrate with us as we commemorate my parent's Golden Anniversary."

A rumble of applause and cheers filled the room, then slowly quieted when it became apparent Vivian had more to say.

"On this very day, fifty years ago, my parents were wed in a beautiful garden in Franklyn, Virginia. We're happy to be joined tonight by Mr. Sumner Lane, one of the wedding guests. Share with us your memories, Mr. Lane."

A stooped elder, aided by a cane, moved next to Vivian. Speaking in a soft voice, he said, "Yes, I remember it well. They hitched up, and after that, we boarded a boat and sailed right down the Black Water River to their family home in Edenton."

"Anything else?" Vivian asked.

He shook his head. "No, that's about the balance of it."

A few titters of laughter sounded, and Vivian smiled. "Thank you, Mr. Sumner." After the elder had returned to his seat, she continued. "I just want to say how much I love my mother and father, and how proud I am of them. Not only are they pillars of this community, but they moved here as the first Black residents of this neighborhood. They paved the way for so many of our best and brightest to live here in the shadow of our nation's capital... such as brilliant writers like Alice and Paul Dunbar. The heroes, like Sergeant Major Fleetwood. The educators, like Mrs. Terrell and Dr. Anna Cooper. They can all call LeDroit Park home, thanks to my mother and father, our guests of honor." She raised her glass high in the air. "Here's to Octavius and Missouri Williams, to fifty years of great love, immense courage, and valuable service. Here's to legacy."

Cheers erupted, glasses were raised and tapped against one another. Maurine smiled, foregoing joining the cacophony so she could focus on her grandparents. She hung back as they shared a soft kiss, then slowly approached the settee. "Happy anniversary, Grandma and Grandpa." Leaning down, she hugged each of them in turn.

Grandma Missy squeezed her hand. "Thank you, sweetheart."

"Yes, we appreciate your regard, Sunshine." Grandpa Octavius smiled, patting his pocket. "I appreciate this spiffy handkerchief, too. Goes real nice with my suit, don't you think?"

She couldn't hold back her grin. "Grandpa, you're so silly sometimes. But you look awfully handsome."

With feigned offense, Grandma Missy placed a hand over the string of pearls at her throat. "What about me? This dress took weeks to make, and I don't even want to consider what it cost. I'm just glad your mother paid."

Maurine giggled. "You look beautiful, Grandma." She elbowed her grandfather gently. "Have you complimented her today, Grandpa?"

He scoffed. "Why, of course. She's still as radiant as the day we wed, and I told her as much." He leaned over and pecked her on the cheek.

Grandma Missy blushed.

Maurine shook her head. *These two. Still canoodling like young lovers.* "Oh, I almost forgot to tell you, Grandpa. I got high marks on my chemistry test."

His delight shone through in his smile. "Excellent job, Sunshine. Keep up those marks, and before you know it, you'll be headed off to Howard."

"Just like Papa, " Maurine added. Part of her worried if she could live up to the legacy of one of the top students to every matriculate through the institution.

"Remember, greatness is in your blood." Grandpa Octavius clasped her hand inside his. "I know women don't often go into doctoring. But you're just as smart and capable as anyone. I know you can follow in your papa's footsteps. Wouldn't be surprised if you outdid him one day."

She looked away; a bit taken aback by the profundity of his words. "I don't know, Grandpa."

He squeezed her hand. "Look at me, Sunshine."

She met his gaze.

Light glimmered in his brown eyes, and he spoke with clarity and conviction. "Maurine Pelham, you will be everything you dream. And don't you ever doubt it. You hear me?"

She nodded, not quite understanding why the tears were stacking up in her throat. Maybe, deep down, she knew she probably didn't have many more years with this amazing, courageous man, who'd loved and guided her since she could remember, who'd always believed in her, even when she couldn't muster any real faith in herself.

She kissed his wrinkled brow. "I heard you, Grandpa. And I promise...I'll never forget."

THE END

Thank you for picking up and reading A CUT ABOVE. It's a busy life and a chaotic world out there, and I appreciate the time you've taken to interact with my book, and to experience the love, courage, and perseverance of Octavius and Missouri Williams. These two unsung heroes of African American history, who paved the way for so many others, are now getting their due acknowledgment and respect.

If you enjoyed the book, please take a moment to review it online at the appropriate retailer site, and/or to post your thoughts on the social site of your choice. Reviews are helpful to authors because they generate buzz and traffic, and are helpful to other readers in determining if a certain book is a fit for them.

Thanks again for reading, reviewing, and supporting. I'm wishing you peace, love, and profound inspiration.

All the Best,

Kianna

AUTHOR'S NOTE

When I wrote *Carolina Built* through 2020 and 2021, I located a lot of tangentially related information which, while I knew it was relevant, I had to set aside. I knew there simply wasn't enough room in the pages of a single book to tell what was quickly becoming a narrative not just about Josephine Leary, but about the legacy of her family line and the remarkable people within.

Due to research on another project about Dr. Anna Julia Haywood Cooper, I was aware of Washington D.C.'s LeDroit Park neighborhood, where Dr. Cooper lived and worked during the early 19th century. The area bears great significance to African American history, due to the extensive list of notable Black figures who have made their home there at one time or another. I was shocked, excited, and touched to discover that Octavius and his wife Missouri had been the first ever Black residents of this storied neighborhood. The courage displayed by the Williamses opened an area that was formerly closed off to Black people, and not just through prevailing attitudes of racism, white supremacy and anti-Blackness. Until action was taken by locals in 1888, as portrayed in the prologue, a fence stood between the exquisite homes of LeDroit Park and the rest of the city.

The Williamses courage in moving into the three-story row house at 338 U. Street NW made it possible for the many other Black residents who would follow them; among them are the best and brightest in art, education, law, literature, and more. It's extremely rare to find this level of talent and intelligence clustered in one place, but LeDroit Park is that place. The Williamses could count 1950 Nobel Peace Prize winner and Harvard PhD Ralph Bunche, poet Paul Laurence Dunbar and his wife, author Alice Dunbar Nelson, and decorated Civil War veteran Sgt. Maj. Christian Fleetwood as their neighbors on U Street. Dr. Cooper, her fellow activist and educator Mary Church Terrell and her husband, the Honorable Robert Terrell and civic leader Walter Washington all made their homes on T Street. This is only a portion of the notable Black residents of LeDroit Park; the bibliography provides additional resources for further information.

In April of 2024, I visited the LeDroit Park neighborhood and took a walking tour. There, I saw the homes of Dr. Cooper, the Dunbar and Terrell homes, as well as the neighboring campus of Howard University. When I arrived at the Williamses home at 338 U Street, where the family lived into the second half of the 20th century, I saw, with my own eyes, the bullet holes in the bricks, a reminder of angry whites who fired guns at the home when they discovered that a Black couple had dared to "sully" their quiet enclave. Layers of white paint and the passage of time could not obscure those distinctive marks. I photographed them, placed my fingertip inside of one. Out of respect for the current owners, I didn't knock on the door, despite my curiosity and desire to see the inside. After what I saw, what I felt as I looked at those bullet holes, and imagined how Octavius and

Missouri must have felt, I left more motivated than ever to write this book.

Readers of CAROLINA BUILT will notice a difference in length compared to this work, A CUT ABOVE is much shorter. At nearly 400 pages, CAROLINA BUILT is representative of the available information, as well as publisher and industry expectations for such a work. With A CUT ABOVE, I was just as purposeful in my approach, though I was free of editorial constraints. I felt this was the best length considering what information is available and can be deduced about the Williamses, and I also hope that the shorter length may attract a broader readership, including those who may have been put off by CAROLINA BUILT's considerable heft. I assure you; I have the same great respect for this story as I did for Mrs. Leary's, and I've poured my efforts into the conception, research, and writing of this book in the same manner.

I've found that readers are often curious about the balance of history and fiction in my novels of this genre. As a demonstration of the balance I've strived to achieve, I've included my research sources in the endnotes. To further demonstrate, I'll list below the true, historically verifiable people and events depicted in A CUT ABOVE.

Real People, Places and Events in
A CUT ABOVE

♦

All members of the Leary/Williams/Pelham family
SAA Richard J. Bright, who hired Octavius at the Capitol
–Members of the US government (Presidents Garfield and McKinley, etc)
Rev. John "Bishop" Sims
Hannibal and Fanny Badham
Paul Laurence Dunbar
Alice Dunbar Nelson
Mary Church Terrell
Robert Terrell
Sgt. Maj. Christian Fleetwood
Thomas E. Waggaman
Charles Bane
The M Street High School (later Dunbar High School)
The Howard Institute (Howard University)
Freedman's Hospital (now Howard University Hospital)
Lipsey's Bar and StoreRoom (and it's owner)
Octavius and Missouri married in Franklyn, Virgina on March 17, 1880.
The LeDroit Park fence was destroyed August 2, 1888.
The Williamses moved into 338 U Street between December 1892 and June 1893.
Vivan was born July 25, 1893.
The *Baltimore Afro-American* reported on the Williamses' Golden Anniversary celebration in the March 22, 1930 edition.

In the interest of telling a compelling story, I have shifted subtle details around these people and events. For example, John "Bishop" Sims actually barbered at the Capitol in the early 20th century, well after Octavius had started there. Generally speaking, I have stuck as closely as possible to the verifiable people, places, and events that make up the story.

I'd like to thank you, the reader, for picking up a copy of A CUT ABOVE. As an author, I have a passion for story-telling that may only be exceeded by my desire to pay due homage and respect to those forgotten, dismissed, or erased figures of African American history. I hope you enjoyed the book, and that if you did, you'll tell a friend or ten. Either way, you have my sincere appreciation for the time you've spent reading this book. May you be inspired, uplifted, and edified by this story of courage, family bonds, and true love.

APPENDIX A: IMAGES

Figure 1: The Williamses on their Golden Anniversary, 1930

Williamses Golden Wedding

The even of the wek, yea, of the years, was the golden wedding anniversary of Mr. and Mrs. Octavius Williams, of 338 U Street, nw., on Monday evening, March 17.

An elaborate reception was given in their honor, by their only daughter, Mrs. Vivian Pelham, the wife of Dr. H. Leroy Pelham, of New York City. Dr. Pelham was unable to attend the reception, due to an emergency operation at the last minute, but he sent his warmest wishes for continued happiness to his wife's parents.

Receiving with Mr. and Mrs. Williams was Mrs. Emma Mahand, a girl-hood friend of Mrs. Williams's, who came from her home in Philadelpnia, to be with her friends on this happy occasion; Mrs. Carrie Lewis. Mrs. Mamie Simms, and Mrs. Mary A. Fearing were also in the receiving line.

Assisting Mrs. Pelham were, her daughter, Miss Maurine Pelham and Miss Margaret Just.

Mr. Sumner Lane recalled interesting details of the wedding, at which he was a guest many years ago, and which took place on St. Patrick's Day of 1880, in Franklyn, Va. The wedding supper, he recalled, was served immediately following the ceremony on the boat, on which the happy bride and groom sailed down the Black Water river to the little town of Edenton, N.C., where they made their home for several years.

Supper was served from a table lovely with gold and cream damask, a centerpiece of brilliant daffodills and tall golden candles.

Among the guests who congratulated Mr. and Mrs. Williams were: Mr. Frank Bright and Mr. Richard Bright, sons of the former sergeant-at-arms, who appointed Mr. Williams to the position at the Capitol, which he held for many years.

Mr. and Mrs. D. B. Evans, Mrs. J. B.

Figure 2: Snippet of Baltimore Afro-American writeup on the Williamses, 1930.

The Le Droit Park Fence Case.

HEARING RESUMED IN THE EQUITY COURT TO-DAY.

In the Equity Court, Judge Cox, this morning, the hearing of Boteler et al., against Barber et al., (the Le Droit Park fence case) was resumed; Messrs. Birney and Birney for complainants and Messrs. Worthington and Heald, for the defendants. Le Droit Park had for years been fenced in and on the north side of the enclosure a number of persons have built houses. In the early part of August, Mr. Bane, agent of Mr. Thos. E. Waggaman, with a force of men, attempted to demolish the fence at Linden street. The complainant filed his bill to restrain the defendants from re-erecting the fence, but before the bond was filed and the temporary order made effective the park people improvised a fence of wire and boards sufficient to prevent the passage of vehicles. The temporary order left the fence in its then condition, and the question now comes up on the motion of defendant's to dissolve the restraining order that defendants may restore the fence to its original condition.

Mr. Birney, in the course of his argument, speaking of the Le Droit Park party, said "they had organized themselves as

WHITE CAPS AND LYNCHERS,

and had endorsed the action of young men in assaulting inoffensive people and preventing them entering the park. We will meet them."

Mr. Worthington—"Pistol with pistol?"

Mr. Birney—"If the court does not take action lives will be lost. The whole thing is an outrage, and I and several others have left the association. As long as it was a law-abiding association I and others stuck to it, but we could not stand such unlawful proceedings as the placing of a man at the fence to bludgeon those who attempt to pass the barrier."

THE INJUNCTION REFUSED.

After Mr. Worthington's closing argument the court dissolved the restraining order and refused the injunction. He said that it was clear the fence having stood so long it should not have been torn down.

Figure 3: Evening Star article about the controversy surrounding the fence.

Figure 4: Historical Map of Ledroit Park.

APPENDIX B: QUESTIONS FOR DISCUSSION

1. What, in your opinion, is the significance of the Williamses decision to leave Edenton? Did you agree or disagree with their choice initially, and did your perspective change as you read?

2. Octavius, like his sister Josephine and his brother-in-law Sweety, was a highly trained and skilled barber; most would consider him a tradesman. By contrast, Octavius' son-in-law, Dr. Harry Pelham, and his granddaughter, Dr. Maurine Pelham Johnson, became noted physicians. Considering the turn of the century debate between W.E.B. Dubois (a proponent of professional education in STEM and other intellectual fields) and Booker T. Washington (who favored training in the trades), how do you think the issue of career choice played out in the lives of the Williams family?

3. Thomas Waggaman and Charles Bane were both wealthy white property investors and developers, who believed LeDroit Park should be open to all. In light of the time period, do you think these men were motivated by the

desire to profit, a genuine desire to help people of color find homes, or something else?

4.   Were you aware of the existence of an exclusive barbershop that caters to the nation's lawmakers? Do you consider the barbershop, which still exists today in a different location, to be a necessary expenditure of taxpayer funds? Is it wasteful, or simply another benefit we provide to ease the burden of such tasks on members of Congress?

5.   What emotions and reactions did you experience to the two scenes where the Williamses experience racist violence? Since historical record and the damage to the structure verifies such events, do you agree or disagree with how Octavius responded, and the ways he attempted to safeguard his home and family?

6.   Howard University is one of the most storied HBCUs in our nation. Both Dr. Pelham and Dr. Johnson attended medical school there, and Dr. Pelham completed his internship at Freedmen's Hospital, now known as Howard University hospital. What influence, if any, do you think the close proximity of this institution to LeDroit Park might have had on its eventual integration?

7.   The Williamses were both North Carolina natives; Octavius was from a plantation in Martin County, while Missouri hailed from Iredell County. Considering their familiarity with more rural settings, do you think they would have experienced difficulty transitioning to the more urban way of life in the nation's capital? Why or why not?

8.   The Capitol Brotherhood, as well as the other three families they invited to live in LeDroit Park, are fictional.

They exist in the absence of information available about who may have assisted the Williamses in their move, coordinated on their behalf, or offered them protection. How do you feel about these plot elements? Do you think such an organization might have actually existed? If not, what are your ideas about how the Williamses were able to move and settle in to their new home, while Missouri was pregnant with Vivian?

9.   What is your opinion of the inclusion of real historical events happening near the main characters, but not necessarily to them, in historical novels? This includes events like President William McKinley's first inauguration, portrayed in Chapter 9. Do these inclusions increase the overall realism of the story for you? Do they distract from the main story? Or do you think they have no significant impact?

10. While most of the homes that were occupied by notable Black residents in LeDroit Park have been identified, and bear some indication of their historical importance through a marker of some kind, no such marker exists at 338 U. Street NW. Given the Williamses role as the first Black residents of the neighborhood, do you believe the home should be acknowledged with such an acknowledgement?

APPENDIX C: SELECTED BIBLIOGRAPHY

"28TH INAUGURAL CEREMONIES." *The Joint Congressional Committee on Inaugural Ceremonies*, 2021, www.inaugural.senate.gov/28th-inaugural-ceremonies/.

"About the Sergeant at Arms: Sergeants at Arms." *U.S. Senate: About the Sergeant at Arms | Sergeants at Arms*, 2025, www.senate.gov/about/officers-staff/sergeant-at-arms/sergeants-at-arms.htm.

"Alice Dunbar Nelson." *Encyclopædia Britannica*, Encyclopædia Britannica, Inc., www.britannica.com/biography/Alice-Dunbar-Nelson.

"April 17 - Together Forever, For Now." *April 17 - Together Forever, For Now | Daily Dunbar*, www.paullaurencedunbar.org/2022/s107.

Ancestry.com. *Washington, D.C., U.S., Select Births and Christenings, 1830-1955* [database on-line]. Provo, UT, USA: Ancestry.com Operations, Inc, 2014.

Ancestry.com. *U.S., Newspapers.com ™ Obituary Index, 1800s-current* [database on-line]. Lehi, UT, USA: Ancestry.com Operations Inc, 2019.

Ancestry.com. *Virginia, U.S., Select Marriages, 1785-1940* [database on-line]. Provo, UT, USA: Ancestry.com Operations, Inc,2014.

Asch, Chris Meyers and Musgrove, George Derek. *Chocolate City*. Chapel Hill, University of North Carolina Press, 2019.

Beauchamp, Tanya Edwards. *Le Droit Park Historic District* (brochure). D.C. Historic Preservation Office. Washington, D.C. Publication Date Unknown.

"Bible Gateway Passage: 2 Chronicles 1:10 - King James Version." *Bible Gateway*, www.biblegateway.com/passage/?search=2+Chronicles+1%3A10&version=KJV.

"DC History Timeline." DC History Center, 10 Dec. 2020, dchistory.org/learn/dchistorytimeline/.

Evening Star. (Washington, DC) 2 Aug. 1888, p. 1. Retrieved from the Library of Congress, www.loc.-gov/item/sn83045462/1888-08-02/ed-1/.

Evening Star. (Washington, DC) 2 Aug. 1888, p. 3. Retrieved from the Library of Congress, www.loc.-gov/item/sn83045462/1888-08-02/ed-1/.

Evening Star. (Washington, DC) 4 Aug. 1888, p. 5. Retrieved from the Library of Congress, www.loc.-gov/item/sn83045462/1888-08-04/ed-1/.

Evening Star. (Washington, DC) 12 Sep. 1888, p. 3. Retrieved from the Library of Congress, www.loc.gov/item/sn83045462/1888-09-12/ed-1/.

Evening Star. (Washington, DC) 11 Feb. 1938, p. 10. Retrieved from the Library of Congress, www.loc.gov/item/sn83045462/1938-02-11/ed-1/.

"Greatest Hits, 1870-85: Variety Music Cavalcade: Articles and Essays: Music for the Nation: American Sheet Music, ca. 1870-1885: Digital Collections: Library of Congress." *The Library of Congress,* www.loc.gov/collections/american-sheet-music-1870-to-1885/articles-and-essays/greatest-hits-1870-85-variety-music-cavalcade/.

"Gun Timeline | History Detectives." *PBS,* Public Broad-casting Service, www.pbs.org/opb/historydetectives/tech-nique/gun-timeline/.

"Howard University Leads Restoration of Historic LeDroit Park Home." *The Dig at Howard University,* thedig.howard.e-du/all-stories/howard-university-leads-restoration-historic-ledroit-park-home.

Image 25, Josephine Napolean Leary Papers (1875-1991), David M. Rubenstein Rare Book & Manuscript Library, Duke University. https://idn.duke.edu/ark:/87924/r4rn33n67

"Inaugural Address." *Inaugural Address | The American Presi-dency Project,* 4 Mar. 1901, www.presidency.ucsb.edu/docu-ments/inaugural-address-44.

Johnson, Wilma J., and Euell A. Dixon. "Alice Ruth Moore

Dunbar-Nelson (1875-1935), 21 May 2022," www.black-past.org/african-american-history/dunbar-nelson-alice-ruth-moore-1875-1935/.

"LeDroit Park Historic District," *African American Heritage Sites* ™, africanamericanheritage-sites.stqry.app/en/story/55556.

Mcclelland, D, J. J Albright, and A.L. Barber And Co. *Plan of LeDroit Park, Washington, D.C.* [Washington? s.n., 188-?, 1880] Map. Retrieved from the Library of Congress, <www.loc.-gov/item/88690892/>.

"Members of the House of Representatives, Fifty-Fourth Congress." *US House of Representatives: History, Art & Archives*, history.house.gov/Collection/Listing/2016/2016-108-000/.

My Dearest Heart, Arthur Sullivan. London: Boosey & Co. [1876] www.gsarchive.net/sullivan/songs/dearest/heart.html.

"North Carolina, United States records," images, Family-Search (https://www.familysearch.org/ark:/61903/3:1:33S7-9RJ4-3GG?view=index : Feb 19, 2025), image 961 of 1103; United States. National Archives and Records Administration.

"Senate Stories: Shaving and Saving: The Story of Bishop Sims." *U.S. Senate: Shaving and Saving: The Story of Bishop Sims,* 16 Sept. 2024, www.senate.gov/artandhistory/senate-stories/Shaving-and-Saving-the-Story-of-Bishop-Sims.htm.

"Square 653 Row Houses." NPS Form 10-900   OMB No. 1024-0018   United States Department of the Interior

National Park Service National Register of Historic Places Registration Form

"The Senate Has Its Own Longstanding, Secretive Basement Barbershop." DCist, 17 June 2019, dcist.com/story/19/06/17/the-senate-has-its-own-secretive-basement-barbershop-that-dates-back-to-the-1800s/.

The Washington times. (Washington [D.C.]), 31 May 1903. *Chronicling America: Historic American Newspapers.* Lib. of Congress. https://chroniclingamerica.loc.gov/lccn/sn84026749/1903-05-31/ed-1/seq-29/

U.S. Census Bureau, "Twelfth Census of the United States," *Population Schedule,* 7-224, U.S. Census Bureau, Washington, DC, 1900

U.S. Census Bureau, "Thirteenth Census of the United States," *Population Schedule,* 185, U.S. Census Bureau, Washington, DC, 1910

U.S. Census Bureau, "Fourteenth Census of the United States," *Population Schedule,* D1-578, U.S. Census Bureau, Washington, DC, 1920

U.S. Census Bureau, "Fifteenth Census of the United States," *Population Schedule,* 15-4, U.S. Census Bureau, Washington, DC, 1930

"United States Presidential Election of 1896." *Encyclopædia Britannica,* Encyclopædia Britannica, Inc., 14 Feb. 2025, www.britannica.com/event/United-States-presidential-election-of-1896. Acce Burns, Judith E. *"Dick" Richard J. Bright - History and Genealogy of Lake Maxinkuckee,* www.maxinkuck-

ee.history.pasttracker.com/maxinkuckee_land-
ing/richard_j_bright.htm.

"Virginia, Marriages, 1785-1940", database, *Family-
Search* (https://familysearch.org/ark:/61903/1:1:XRMF-7X4
: 29 January 2020), Santoria A. Leigh in entry for Percy A.
R..., 1928.

"Washington DC Historic Sites." *Soul Of America*, 1 Nov.
2024, www.soulofamerica.com/us-cities/washington-
dc/washington-dc-historic-sites/.

APPENDIX D: CAROLINA BUILT

This "exuberant celebration of Black women's joy as well
as their achievements" (Kate Quinn, *New York
Times* bestselling author) novelizes the life of real estate
magnate Josephine N. Leary in a previously untold story

of passion, perseverance, and building a legacy after emancipation in North Carolina.

Josephine N. Leary is determined to build a life of her own and a future for her family. When she moves to Edenton, North Carolina, from the plantation where she was born, she is free, newly married, and ready to follow her dreams.

As the demands of life pull Josephine's attention away, it becomes increasingly difficult for her to pursue her real estate aspirations. She finds herself immersed in deepening her marriage, mothering her daughters, and being a dutiful daughter and granddaughter. Still, she manages to teach herself to be a businesswoman, to manage her finances, and to make smart investments in the local real estate market. But with each passing year, it grows more and more difficult to focus on building her legacy from the ground up.

"Filled with passion and perseverance, Josephine Leary is frankly a woman that everyone should know" (Sadeqa Johnson, author of *Yellow Wife*) and her story speaks to the part of us that dares to dream bigger, tear down whatever stands in our way, and build something better for the loved ones we leave behind.

Carolina Built **is available wherever books are sold. Check out <u>Bookshop.org</u> for independent bookseller options.**

APPENDIX E: COMING SOON

COMPASSION ON CALL: The VA's Dr. Johnson

Dr. Maurine Pelham Johnson

Figure 5: From a 1965 Washington Post article about Dr. Johnson.

The untold story of a Black woman rising from a working-class background in Washington DC at the turn of the 20th century, to a storied medical career caring for American's veterans that would place her in a position of authority over more than 270 healthcare professionals.

From the author of the North Carolina Humanities/ National Endowment for Humanities 2023 Book Club pick CAROLINA BUILT comes another true and remarkable tale of excellence, determination, and perseverance in the face of massive opposition, straight from the Williams/Leary family line.

~

COMPASSION ON CALL tells the real-life story of Dr. Maurine P. Johnson, the great-niece of **CAROLINA BUILT** heroine, businesswoman and real estate developer Josephine Napoleon Williams Leary, and the granddaughter of **A CUT ABOVE: The Williamses Integrate D.C.'s LeDroit Park**'s main characters, Octavius and Missouri Williams.

Maurine, raised in a middle-class family by a doctor and a homemaker, graduated from two of Washington DC's most storied Black institutions: Dunbar High and Howard University, and would go on to reach the rank of Chief of Staff at the District's Veterans Administration Hospital during the pivotal transitional period from the Civil Rights era to the rise of the Black Power movement. Set primarily in early 20th Century Washington, DC, (with special focus on LeDroit Park) the narrative will follow Dr. Johnson's life and career through other locations including Detroit, Michigan and Dayton, Ohio.

Dr. Johnson's life, spent in pursuit of learning, healing, and providing empathetic care for America's service members returning home from distant battlefields, is a testament to the importance of equal access to educational opportunity, and gives credence to the notion that excellence can be passed down through a bloodline, from one generation to the next.

COMPASSION ON CALL is currently in the works! You won't want to miss this continuation of the Williams/Leary family saga. For updates, including ARC availability, pre-order, and related events, go to www.KiannaAlexanderWrites.com and scroll to the "Mailing List Signup" icon.

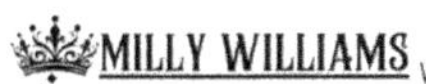

MILLY WILLIAMS — May 12, 1807-July 16, 1906
Williamston, NC- Edenton, NC

**Jeanette's father is unknown.*

JEANETTE WILLIAMS
1840-c 1910
Williamston, NC-Edenton NC

DORSEY STEWART
1837-????
North Carolina
Married November 10, 1873, Edenton NC

**Jeanette's children, Jospehine and Octavius, were
likely fathered by a white man, Col. William Lamb,
a Confederate officer from Norfolk, VA. We can safely
assume these encounters were non-consensual (rape).*

JOSEPHINE NAPOLEON WILLIAMS
April 1856-March 13, 1923
Williamston, NC-Edenton, NC

OCTAVIUS AUGUSTUS WILLIAMS
December 1858-March 2, 1936
Williamston, NC-Washington, DC

SWEETY ARCHER LEARY
Married 1872- Elizabeth City, NC
1850-c. 1909
Petersburg, VA-Edenton, NC

MISSOURI ARMSTRONG BENBURY
Married March 17, 1880-
Franklyn, VA
December 1859-February 10, 1938
Iredell Co, NC-Washington, D.C.

CLARA LEARY
April 7, 1874- October 17, 1939
Edenton, NC
**Clara was married and widowed three times.*

FLORENCE J. LEARY
March 1880-????
Edenton, NC- ????

"GRAVES"

JAMES H. REEVES
Married 1895
1873-1905

GING JUNG
Married between 1920-1923
????-????
China- ????

UNKNOWN/
CHILDREN POSSIBLE

VIVIAN WILLIAMS
July 25, 1893-late 1940s
Washington, D.C.

NOAH C. RYAN
Married c. 1915
1856- December, 1932

FRANK REEVES
Married July 1935
1867-January 1936

HAROLD LEROY PELHAM, M.D.
Married Early 1915
February 28, 1892-March 22, 1985
Newburgh,NY-Washington, D.C.

PERCIVAL ALMERIA REEVES
August 7, 1897-April 30, 1994
Edenton, NC-Hertford, NC

MAURINE PELHAM, M.D.
June 15, 1915-December 3, 2000
Washington, D.C.

"WEAVER" m. ???? 1940-Winston Salem, NC

JAMES REDDEN m. October 17, 1944 March 29, 1950

SANTORIA LEIGH
Married April 8, 1928- Norfolk, VA
January 5, 1907-August 6, 1971
Washington, DC- Edenton, NC

NO CHILDREN

SGT. WILLIAM JOHNSON
Married May 5, 1951-Indiana
March 1917-April 1989
Kentucky-Washington, D.C.

NO CHILDREN

WILLIAMS/LEARY FAMILY TREE

MARRIAGE

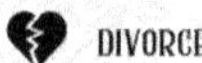
DIVORCE

CHILD WHO LIVE TO MATURITY

Like any good Southern belle, Kianna Alexander wears many hats: doting mama, advice-dispensing sister, fun aunt and gabbing girlfriend. She's a voracious reader, an amateur seamstress and occasional painter in oils. She has a passion for history and an endless curiosity. Kianna is proud to tell stories where Black women are loved, valued, and thriving. A native of the TarHeel state, Kianna still lives there while maintaining her collection of well-loved vintage 80's Barbie dolls.

Find out more about Kianna and her books by visiting her website at KiannaAlexanderWrites.com.